The Lovely Bones

(Best Edition of the Year)

Chapter

1

all kids, besides one, expand up. They quick recognise that they may develop up, and the way wendy knew emerge as this. Finally when she changed into years vintage she was gambling in a garden, and she plucked a few other flower and ran with it to her mother. I assume she have to have appeared rather nice, for mrs. Darling positioned her hand to her coronary heart and cried, "oh, why can not you stay like this for ever!" this became all that surpassed among them on the difficulty, however henceforth wendy knew that she ought to develop up. You continuously comprehend once you are two. Is the begin of the stop. Of path they lived at 14 [their house number on their street], and till wendy got here her mom changed into the chief one. She come to be a lovely female, with a romantic mind and this kind of candy mocking mouth. Her romantic thoughts changed into just like the tiny boxes, one within the exclusive, that come from the perplexing east, however many you discover there is usually one extra; and her candy mocking mouth had one kiss on it that wendy can also want to never get, even though there it modified into, flawlessly conspicuous within the proper-hand corner. The manner mr. Darling obtained her become this: the severa gentlemen who were boys even as she become a girl determined simultaneously that they loved her, and all of them ran to her house to advocate to her except mr. Darling, who took a cab and nipped in first, and so he were given her. He have been given all of her, besides the innermost field and the kiss. He never knew approximately the field, and in time he gave up trying for the kiss. Wendy concept napoleon must have were given it, but i am able to photograph him attempting, after which going off in a ardour, slamming the door. Mr. Darling used to boast to wendy that her mother not first-rate loved him but respected him. He become this kind of deep ones who know approximately stocks and shares. Of direction no man or woman genuinely knows, however he pretty appeared to understand, and he frequently said shares have been up and stocks had been down in a manner that would have made any girl admire him. Mrs. Darling became married in white, and earlier than everything she saved the books perfectly, nearly gleefully, as though it have been a recreation, no longer lots as a brussels sprout end up missing; however by means of the use of and with the useful resource of whole cauliflowers dropped out, and in region of them there had been photos of infants with out faces. She drew them whilst she need to had been totting up. They were mrs. Darling's guesses. Wendy came first, then john, then michael. For every week or after wendy got here it became dubious whether or not or now not they might be able to maintain her, as she come to be every other mouth to feed. Mr. Darling end up frightfully pleased with her, but he changed into very honourable, and he sat on the point of mrs. Darling's bed, preserving her hand and calculating fees, whilst she looked at him imploringly. She favored to risk it, come what could possibly, but that changed into now not his way; his manner modified into with a pencil and a bit of paper, and if she harassed him with hints he had to begin at the start again.

"now don't interrupt," he would beg of her.

"i've one pound seventeen proper here, and and six on the place of work; i can lessen off my espresso at the place of job, say ten shillings, making two 9 and 6, along with your eighteen and 3 makes 3 9 seven, with 5 naught naught in my cheque-ebook makes 8 nine seven—who's that moving?—8 9 seven, dot and bring seven—do not speak, my very own—and the pound you lent to that guy who came to the door—quiet, infant—dot and deliver infant—there, you've got completed it!—did i say 9 9 seven? Sure, i stated nine 9 seven; the query is, can we attempt it for a 12 months on 9 nine seven?"

"of route we will, george," she cried. However she have become prejudiced in wendy's favour, and he changed into in reality the grander man or woman of the two.

"consider mumps," he warned her almost threateningly, and off he went once more. "mumps one pound, that's what i've placed down, but i daresay it'll be extra like thirty shillings—don't talk—measles one 5, german measles 1/2 a guinea, makes fifteen six—do now not waggle your finger—whooping-cough, say fifteen shillings"—and so forth it went, and it introduced up differently each time; but at remaining wendy just were given through, with mumps decreased to 12 six, and the 2 styles of measles dealt with as one. There has been the equal pride over john, and michael had even a narrower squeak; however both were kept, and soon, you can have seen the three of them entering into a row to miss fulsom's kindergarten faculty, located via their nurse. Mrs. Darling cherished to have everything simply so, and mr. Darling had a passion for being exactly like his neighbours; so, of route, they'd a nurse. As they were poor, due to the quantity of milk the youngsters drank, this nurse became a prim newfoundland dog, referred to as nana, who had belonged to no character specially until the darlings engaged her. She had usually concept kids crucial, but, and the darlings had end up familiar along side her in kensington gardens, in which she spent most of her spare time peeping into perambulators, and have become masses hated through careless nursemaids, whom she observed to their houses and complained of to their mistresses. She proved to be quite a treasure of a nurse. How thorough she became at bath-time, and up at any 2d of the night time if taken into consideration considered one of her charges made the slightest cry. Of path her kennel changed into inside the nursery. She had a genius for understanding at the same time as a cough is a aspect to don't have any patience with and at the same time as it desires stocking round your throat. She believed to her closing day in old fashioned remedies like rhubarb leaf, and made sounds of contempt over all this new-fangled talk approximately germs, and so on. It became a lesson in propriety to appearance her escorting the youngsters to school, taking walks sedately by using their facet when they were properly behaved, and butting them lower back into line inside the occasion that they strayed. On john's footer [in england soccer was called football, "footer" for short] days she in no way as soon as forgot his sweater, and she or he or he commonly carried an umbrella in her mouth in case of rain. There's a room inside the basement of omit fulsom's university in which the nurses wait. They sat on office work, at the same time as nana lay at the ground, however that became the most effective difference. They affected to disregard her as of an inferior social status to themselves, and he or she despised their mild communicate. She resented visits to the nursery from mrs. Darling's friends, however if they did come she first whipped off michael's pinafore and placed him into the simplest with blue braiding, and smoothed out wendy and made a dash at john's hair. No nursery could in all likelihood were accomplished more efficiently, and mr. Darling knew it, yet he every so often perplexed uneasily whether or now not the neighbours talked. He had his role in the town to bear in mind. Nana moreover him in another way. He had on occasion a feel that she did not recognize him. "i understand she admires you fairly, george," mrs. Darling could assure him, and then she could signal to the kids to be in particular first-class to father. Adorable dances followed, wherein the handiest extraordinary servant, liza, modified into now and again allowed to join. This type of midget she looked in her lengthy skirt and maid's cap, despite the fact that she had sworn, when engaged, that she could in no way see ten once more. The gaiety of those romps! And gayest of all was mrs. Darling, who might pirouette so wildly that all you can see of her was the kiss, and then if you had dashed at her you could have were given it. There by no means became a simpler happier own family until the approaching of peter pan. Mrs. Darling first heard of peter at the same time as she changed into tidying up her children's minds. It is the nightly custom of every desirable mother after her kids are asleep to rummage of their minds and positioned matters right now for next morning, repacking into their proper locations the various articles which have wandered at some degree inside the day. If you may maintain awake (however of route you cannot) you'll see your own mother doing this, and you'll find it very exciting to have a look at her. It's miles pretty like tidying up drawers. You will see her on her knees, i count on, lingering humorously over a number of your contents, thinking in which on the planet you had picked this element up, making discoveries sweet and no longer so sweet, urgent this to her cheek as though it were as exceptional as a kitten, and hurriedly stowing that out of sight. Even as you wake inside the morning, the naughtiness and evil passions with that you went to mattress had been folded up small and positioned at the lowest of your mind and on the top, quite aired, are unfold out your prettier mind, geared up in case you want to position on. I do not know whether or not you have got got ever seen a map of a person's mind. Scientific doctors every now and then draw maps of different elements of you, and your very own map can grow to be intensely interesting, but capture them in search of to draw a map of a toddler's thoughts, which isn't first-rate harassed, however maintains going round all of the time. There are zigzag lines on it, similar to your temperature on a card, and those are possibly roads inside the island, for the neverland is normally more or a lot less an island, with first-rate splashes of shade proper here and there, and coral reefs and rakish-searching craft inside the offing, and savages and lonely lairs, and gnomes who're in maximum cases tailors, and caves via which a river runs, and princes with six elder brothers, and a hut rapid going to decay, and one very small vintage female with a hooked nose. It might be an clean map if that have been all, however there's also first day at university, religion, fathers, the round pond, needle-paintings, murders, hangings, verbs that take the dative, chocolate pudding day, getting into braces, say ninety-nine, three-pence for pulling out your teeth your self, and so forth, and both these are a part of the island or they're a few different map displaying via, and it's far all instead puzzling, mainly as not some thing will stand however. Of route the neverlands range a good deal. John's, as an instance, had a lagoon with flamingoes flying over it at which john emerge as taking snap shots, at the identical time as michael, who modified into very small, had a flamingo with lagoons flying over it. John lived in a boat grew to come to be the other way up on the sands, michael in a wigwam, wendy in a residence of leaves deftly sewn collectively. John had no buddies, michael had buddies at night, wendy had a pup wolf forsaken by using its dad and mom, however on the complete the neverlands have a circle of relatives resemblance, and if they stood despite the fact that in a row you could say of them that they've each different's nostril, and so forth. On these magic seashores children at play are for ever beaching their coracles [simple boat]. We too had been there; we're capable of though listen the sound of the surf, although we shall land no greater. Of all delectable islands the neverland is the snuggest and most compact, not large and sprawly, you recognize, with tedious distances among one journey and each different, but well stuffed. While you play at it thru day with the chairs and desk-cloth, it isn't inside the least alarming, however in the two mins earlier than you fall asleep it becomes very real. This is why there are night time time-lighting fixtures. Every so often in her travels thru her children's minds mrs. Darling found topics she couldn't understand, and of those pretty the maximum confusing changed into the phrase peter. She knew of no peter, and however he have become right here and there in john and michael's minds, at the same time as wendy's started out out to be scrawled all over with him. The call stood out in bolder letters than any of the alternative phrases, and as mrs. Darling gazed she felt that it had an oddly cocky look.

"sure, he's alternatively cocky," wendy admitted with regret. Her mother were questioning her.

"however who is he, my doggy?"

"he is peter pan, , mother."

at the start mrs. Darling did now not realise, however after wondering decrease back into her youth she simply remembered a peter pan who changed into stated to stay with the fairies. There have been regular stories approximately him, as that once children died he went part of the way with them, simply so they ought to now not be apprehensive. She had believed in him on the time, however now that she become married and full of sense she quite doubted whether or now not there has been this type of person.

"except," she stated to wendy, "he would be grown up by using this time."

"oh no, he isn't always grown up," wendy assured her with a bit of luck, "and he's just my duration." she meant that he became her length in each mind and frame; she failed to realize how she knew, she virtually knew it. Mrs. Darling consulted mr. Darling, however he smiled pooh-pooh. "mark my phrases," he said, "it is a few nonsense nana has been setting into their heads; surely the type of idea a dog could have. Leave it on my own, and it'll blow over."

but it'd now not blow over and shortly the tough boy gave mrs. Darling quite a shock. Kids have the strangest adventures without being troubled with the useful resource of them. For example, they will bear in mind to mention, per week after the event happened, that when they had been in the timber they'd met their lifeless father and had a pastime with him. It end up on this informal manner that wendy one morning made a disquieting revelation. A few leaves of a tree were found on the nursery ground, which clearly have been no longer there at the same time as the kids went to mattress, and mrs. Darling come to be hard over them whilst wendy said with a tolerant smile:

"i do agree with it's far that peter yet again!"

"whatever do you imply, wendy?"

"it is so naughty of him not to wipe his ft," wendy stated, sighing. She changed right into a tidy baby. She defined in quite a count number-of-reality manner that she notion peter occasionally came to the nursery inside the night and sat on the foot of her mattress and carried out on his pipes to her. Lamentably she in no way woke, so she did not understand how she knew, she simply knew.

"what nonsense you speak, treasured. No person can get into the house without knocking."

"i expect he comes in by using the window," she said.

"my love, it's miles three flooring up."

"have been now not the leaves on the foot of the window, mother?"

it changed into pretty right; the leaves had been determined very near the window. Mrs. Darling did not apprehend what to count on, for all of it seemed so herbal to wendy which you could not brush aside it by means of way of pronouncing she have been dreaming.

"my infant," the mother cried, "why did you now not inform me of this in advance than?"

"i forgot," stated wendy gently. She grow to be in a hurry to get her breakfast. Oh, in fact she must have been dreaming. However, however, there were the leaves. Mrs. Darling examined them very cautiously; they had been skeleton leaves, but she have become sure they did not come from any tree that grew in england. She crawled about the floor, peering at it with a candle for marks of a ordinary foot. She rattled the poker up the chimney and tapped the walls. She permit down a tape from the window to the pavement, and it modified into a sheer drop of thirty toes, with out a lot as a spout to climb up with the aid of. Definitely wendy were dreaming. But wendy had now not been dreaming, because the very next night time confirmed, the night on which the awesome adventures of those kids may be stated to have all began. At the night time we speak of all of the children were yet again in mattress. It happened to be nana's night time off, and mrs. Darling had bathed them and sung to them until one after the other they'd permit bypass her hand and slid away into the land of sleep. All have been searching so safe and relaxed that she smiled at her fears now and sat down tranquilly via the fireplace to sew. It changed into some thing for michael, who on his birthday turned into getting into shirts. The fireplace was warmth, however, and the nursery dimly lit through three night time-lighting, and currently the sewing lay on mrs. Darling's lap. Then her head nodded, oh, so gracefully. She modified into asleep. Examine the 4 of them, wendy and michael over there, john proper here, and mrs. Darling with the aid of the hearth. There need to were a fourth night time-mild. While she slept she had a dream. She dreamt that the neverland had come too close to and that a odd boy had broken thru from it. He did no longer alarm her, for she perception she had seen him in advance than inside the faces of many ladies who've no children. In all likelihood he's to be determined in the faces of some moms additionally. But in her dream he had hire the movie that obscures the neverland, and she or he observed wendy and john and michael peeping via the distance. The dream via way of itself might have been a trifle, but even as she became dreaming the window of the nursery blew open, and a boy did drop at the floor. He became accompanied by means of a notable slight, no larger than your fist, which darted approximately the room like a dwelling factor and i expect it need to have been this light that awoke mrs. Darling. She commenced out up with a cry, and observed the boy, and are available what may additionally she knew straight away that he modified into peter pan. In case you or i or wendy have been there we must have seen that he became very like mrs. Darling's kiss. He became a adorable boy, clad in skeleton leaves and the juices that ooze out of timber however the most entrancing issue about him changed into that he

had all his first enamel. While he noticed she come to be a grown-up, he gnashed the little pearls at her.
Chapter

Chapter 2

mrs. Darling screamed, and, as though in approach to a bell, the door opened, and nana entered, returned from her night out. She growled and sprang on the boy, who leapt gently through the window. Once more mrs. Darling screamed, this time in misery for him, for she notion he have become killed, and she or he ran down into the road to search for his little body, but it became now not there; and she appeared up, and inside the black night time she ought to see nothing however what she perception grow to be a taking pictures big name. She again to the nursery, and observed nana with some thing in her mouth, which proved to be the boy's shadow. As he leapt at the window nana had closed it speedy, too late to seize him, however his shadow had no longer had time to get out; slam went the window and snapped it off. You will be nice mrs. Darling tested the shadow cautiously, but it became pretty the everyday kind. Nana had absolute confidence of what turned into the brilliant element to do with this shadow. She hung it out at the window, meaning "he's sure to return decrease again for it; allow us to placed it wherein he can get it with out issues with out stressful the kids."

however unfortunately mrs. Darling couldn't depart it placing out on the window, it appeared so just like the bathing and diminished the entire tone of the house. She notion of showing it to mr. Darling, however he modified into totting up winter remarkable-coats for john and michael, with a moist towel round his head to maintain his brain smooth, and it regarded a disgrace to trouble him; except, she knew exactly what he ought to say: "all of it comes of getting a dog for a nurse."

she determined to roll the shadow up and positioned it away cautiously in a drawer, till a turning into possibility got here for telling her husband. Ah me! The possibility came each week later, on that in no manner-to-be-forgotten friday. Of course it become a friday.

"i need to were especially cautious on a friday," she used to mention afterwards to her husband, whilst perhaps nana changed into at the alternative aspect of her, preserving her hand.

"no, no," mr. Darling continually stated, "i am answerable for all of it. I, george darling, did it. Mea culpa, mea culpa." he had had a classical training. They sat consequently night after night time recalling that deadly friday, till every element of it grow to be stamped on their brains and got here via on the alternative factor much like the faces on a awful coinage.

"if most effective i had now not widely wide-spread that invitation to dine at 27," mrs. Darling said.

"if handiest i had no longer poured my medicinal drug into nana's bowl," said mr. Darling.

"if satisfactory i had pretended to like the medication," have become what nana's wet eyes said.

"my liking for events, george."

"my deadly gift of humour, dearest."

"my touchiness about trifles, highly-priced hold close and mistress."

then one or greater of them might ruin down altogether; nana at the perception, "it is proper, it is true, they ought not to have had a canine for a nurse." many a time it changed into mr. Darling who located the handkerchief to nana's eyes.

"that fiend!" mr. Darling may cry, and nana's bark emerge as the echo of it, however mrs. Darling in no manner upbraided peter; there was some thing inside the right-hand nook of her mouth that desired her no longer to name peter names. They could sit down there within the empty nursery, recalling fondly every smallest element of that dreadful evening. It had all started so uneventfully, so exactly like a hundred other evenings, with nana placing on the water for michael's bathtub and carrying him to it on her again.

"i won't go to mattress," he had shouted, like person who though believed that he had the last word on the concern, "i won't, i might not. Nana, it isn't always six o'clock however. Oh steeply-priced, oh luxurious, i shan't love you any greater, nana. I allow you to understand i may not be bathed, i may not, i won't!"

then mrs. Darling had are to be had in, carrying her white nighttime-robe. She had dressed early because of the truth wendy so cherished to look her in her night-gown, with the necklace george had given her. She grow to be wearing wendy's bracelet on her arm; she had requested for the mortgage of it. Wendy cherished to lend her bracelet to her mom. She had placed her two older kids gambling at being herself and father on the occasion of wendy's start, and john turned into pronouncing:

"i'm glad to inform you, mrs. Darling, which you for the time being are a mom," in just this type of tone as mr. Darling himself may additionally moreover have used on the actual event. Wendy had danced with pleasure, simply as the real mrs. Darling must have completed. Then john was born, with the greater pomp that he conceived due to the delivery of a male, and michael came from his bathtub to invite to be born additionally, however john stated brutally that they did now not need any greater. Michael had nearly cried. "no person needs me," he stated, and of path the woman in the night time-dress couldn't stand that.

"i do," she said, "i so want a 3rd toddler."

"boy or female?" requested michael, now not too optimistically.

"boy."

then he had leapt into her arms. One of these little component for mr. And mrs. Darling and nana to endure in thoughts now, however no longer so little if that changed into to be michael's final night in the nursery. They pass on with their reminiscences.

"it end up then that i rushed in like a twister, wasn't it?" mr. Darling may want to say, scorning himself; and certainly he have been like a tornado. Probable there was a few excuse for him. He, too, have been dressing for the birthday party, and all had lengthy beyond properly with him till he got here to his tie. It's miles an astounding thing to have to inform, however this man, though he knew about shares and stocks, had no actual mastery of his tie. Sometimes the element yielded to him without a opposition, but there had been activities at the same time as it'd have been better for the house if he had swallowed his satisfaction and used a made-up tie. This changed into such an event. He came rushing into the nursery with the crumpled little brute of a tie in his hand.

"why, what's the hassle, father expensive?"

"count!" he yelled; he certainly yelled. "this tie, it's going to now not tie." he became dangerously sarcastic. "no longer spherical my neck! Round the bed-put up! Oh sure, twenty instances have i made it up spherical the bed-put up, however spherical my neck, no! Oh costly no! Begs to be excused!"

he idea mrs. Darling end up now not sufficiently impressed, and he went on sternly, "i provide you with a warning of this, mom, that except this tie is round my neck we do no longer exit to dinner to-night time time, and if i do not go out to dinner to-night time time, i never visit the workplace once more, and if i do not visit the office once more, you and that i starve, and our children may be flung into the streets."

even then mrs. Darling turn out to be placid. "permit me strive, luxurious," she stated, and indeed that modified into what he had come to invite her to do, and with her fine cool hands she tied his tie for him, even as the kids stood spherical to see their future decided. Some men should have resented her being able to do it so without trouble, however mr. Darling had some distance too outstanding a nature for that; he thanked her carelessly, at once forgot his rage, and in some other moment turn out to be dancing spherical the room with michael on his lower back.

"how wildly we romped!" says mrs. Darling now, recalling it.

"our ultimate romp!" mr. Darling groaned.

"o george, do you consider michael unexpectedly said to me, 'how did you get to recognize me, mom?'"

"i consider!"

"they were as an alternative candy, do not you suspect, george?"

"and they were ours, ours! And now they're lengthy beyond."

the romp had ended with the arrival of nana, and most alas mr. Darling collided in the direction of her, protective his trousers with hairs. They were now not first-class new trousers, however they had been the primary he had ever had with braid on them, and he had needed to chew his lip to save you the tears coming. Of route mrs. Darling brushed him, but he commenced to speak over again approximately its being a mistake to have a canine for a nurse.

"george, nana is a treasure."

"no doubt, however i've an uneasy feeling at instances that she seems upon the kids as dogs."

"oh no, costly one, i feel certain she knows they've souls."

"i wonder," mr. Darling stated thoughtfully, "i ponder." it modified into an opportunity, his spouse felt, for telling him about the boy. Inside the beginning he pooh-poohed the story, however he have end up considerate even as she showed him the shadow.

"it's miles nobody i realise," he stated, inspecting it cautiously, "but it does appearance a scoundrel."

"we had been though discussing it, you hold in mind," says mr. Darling, "at the same time as nana got here in with michael's remedy. You may in no way carry the bottle on your mouth once more, nana, and it's far all my fault."

robust guy even though he become, there can be no question that he had behaved instead foolishly over the medicine. If he had a vulnerable factor, it have become for wondering that all his life he had taken remedy boldly, and so now, even as michael dodged the spoon in nana's mouth, he had said reprovingly, "be a person, michael."

"might not; might not!" michael cried naughtily. Mrs. Darling left the room to get a chocolate for him, and mr. Darling perception this confirmed need of firmness.

"mom, do not pamper him," he referred to as after her. "michael, at the same time as i was your age i took medicine without a murmur. I said, 'thank you, kind dad and mom, for giving me bottles to make we nicely.'"

he without a doubt concept this turn out to be right, and wendy, who become now in her night-robe, believed it additionally, and she or he or he said, to encourage michael, "that remedy you every so often take, father, is a great deal nastier, is not it?"

"ever so much nastier," mr. Darling said bravely, "and i might take it now as an example to you, michael, if i hadn't lost the bottle."

he had no longer precisely lost it; he had climbed inside the lifeless of night time to the pinnacle of the wardrobe and hidden it there. What he did now not apprehend modified into that the sincere liza had decided it, and positioned it again on his wash-stand.

"i understand in which it's miles, father," wendy cried, always happy to be of carrier. "i can carry it," and she turned into off earlier than he could stop her. Straight away his spirits sank inside the strangest manner.

"john," he said, shuddering, "it's maximum beastly stuff. It is that nasty, sticky, sweet type."

"it will speedy be over, father," john said cheerily, after which in rushed wendy with the medicine in a tumbler.

"i've been as brief as i could," she panted.

"you have got were given been wonderfully quick," her father retorted, with a vindictive politeness that changed into pretty thrown away upon her. "michael first," he stated doggedly.

"father first," said michael, who end up of a suspicious nature.

"i might be ill, you recognize," mr. Darling stated threateningly.

"come on, father," stated john.

"hold your tongue, john," his father rapped out. Wendy changed into quite perplexed. "i idea you took it pretty without difficulty, father."

"that is not the factor," he retorted. "the point is, that there is extra in my glass than in michael's spoon." his proud heart was almost bursting. "and it isn't honest: i might say it even though it have been with my ultimate breath; it isn't sincere."

"father, i'm ready," stated michael coldly.

"it is all very well to mention you are prepared; so am i ready."

"father's a cowardly custard."

"so are you a cowardly custard."

"i am not apprehensive."

"neither am i nervous."

"well, then, take it."

"nicely, then, you take it."

wendy had a super idea. "why now not both take it at the equal time?"

"in fact," said mr. Darling. "are you ready, michael?"

wendy gave the words, one, , three, and michael took his treatment, but mr. Darling slipped his in the back of his once more. There was a yell of rage from michael, and "o father!" wendy exclaimed.

"what do you imply by means of 'o father'?" mr. Darling demanded. "stop that row, michael. I intended to take mine, however i—i neglected it."

it changed into dreadful the manner all of the 3 had been searching at him, clearly as though they did not respect him. "look proper here, all of you," he said entreatingly, as quickly as nana had long gone into the toilet. "i have absolutely belief of a brilliant shaggy dog story. I shall pour my remedy into nana's bowl, and she or he will drink it, questioning it is milk!"

it have become the shade of milk; however the kids did now not have their father's sense of humour, and they looked at him reproachfully as he poured the medication into nana's bowl. "what fun!" he said doubtfully, and that they did now not dare display him when mrs. Darling and nana again.

"nana, suitable canine," he said, patting her, "i have positioned a touch milk into your bowl, nana."

nana wagged her tail, ran to the medication, and started out lapping it. Then she gave mr. Darling one of these appearance, now not an irritated appearance: she showed him the fantastic purple tear that makes us so sorry for noble puppies, and crept into her kennel. Mr. Darling changed into frightfully ashamed of himself, but he may not deliver in. In a horrid silence mrs. Darling smelt the bowl. "o george," she stated, "it is your medication!"

"it have become handiest a funny story," he roared, on the equal time as she comforted her boys, and wendy hugged nana. "lots appropriate," he said bitterly, "my carrying myself to the bone looking to be humorous in this residence."

and however wendy hugged nana. "it simply is proper," he shouted. "coddle her! No man or woman coddles me. Oh expensive no! I am simplest the breadwinner, why have to i be coddled—why, why, why!"

"george," mrs. Darling counseled him, "no longer so loud; the servants will pay attention you." come what may additionally they had have been given into the manner of calling liza the servants.

"let them!" he replied recklessly. "convey in the whole international. However i refuse to allow that canine to lord it in my nursery for an hour longer."

the youngsters wept, and nana ran to him beseechingly, however he waved her again. He felt he have become a sturdy man again. "in vain, in vain," he cried; "the proper location for you is the backyard, and there you go to be tied up this immediate."

"george, george," mrs. Darling whispered, "don't forget what i informed you approximately that boy."

sadly, he might now not listen. He turned into determined to reveal who became draw close in that house, and at the same time as commands would no longer draw nana from the kennel, he lured her out of it with honeyed terms, and seizing her sort of, dragged her from the nursery. He become ashamed of himself, and but he did it. It became all owing to his too affectionate nature, which craved for admiration. While he had tied her up within the once more-yard, the wretched father went and sat in the passage, alongside together with his knuckles to his eyes. Within the period in-between mrs. Darling had positioned the kids to bed in unwonted silence and lit their night time-lighting. They could pay attention nana barking, and john whimpered, "it's miles due to the fact he's chaining her up in the yard," but wendy become wiser.

"that isn't nana's unhappy bark," she said, little guessing what became about to take place; "that is her bark whilst she smells chance."

hazard!

"are you fantastic, wendy?"

"oh, yes."

mrs. Darling quivered and went to the window. It turned into securely fastened. She regarded out, and the night time turned into peppered with stars. They have been crowding round the residence, as if curious to look what become to take location there, however she did not examine this, nor that one or of the smaller ones winked at her. However a anonymous fear clutched at her heart and made her cry, "oh, how i wish that i wasn't going to a celebration to-night time time!"

even michael, already 1/2 asleep, knew that she have become perturbed, and he asked, "can whatever harm us, mom, after the night-lighting are lit?"

"not whatever, precious," she stated; "they're the eyes a mother leaves at the back of her to protect her kids."

she went from bed to mattress making a tune enchantments over them, and little michael flung his palms round her. "mother," he cried, "i am satisfied of you." they were the final phrases she end up to hear from him for a long time. No. 27 turned into only a few yards distant, but there have been a mild fall of snow, and parents darling picked their way over it deftly now not to soil their shoes. They had been already the great people in the road, and all of the stars had been searching them. Stars are stunning, however they will no longer take an energetic factor in whatever, they ought to honestly appearance on for ever. It's far a punishment placed on them for some thing they did good-bye in the past that no celeb now knows what it emerge as. So the older ones have end up glassy-eyed and seldom communicate (winking is the celebrity language), however the little ones however surprise. They're now not really first-class to peter, who had a mischievous manner of stealing up at the back of them and looking for to blow them out; but they're so eager on amusing that they have been on his facet to-night time time, and disturbing to get the grown-u. S. Out of the manner. In order soon because the door of 27 closed on mr. And mrs. Darling there was a commotion in the firmament, and the smallest of all of the stars within the milky way screamed out:

"now, peter!"

Chapter 3

come away, come away! For a second after mr. And mrs. Darling left the residence the night-lighting with the resource of the beds of the 3 children persevered to burn surely. They have been quite pleasant little night time-lights, and one cannot assist wishing that they may have stored wide awake to peer peter; but wendy's slight blinked and gave any such yawn that the alternative yawned additionally, and earlier than they could close to their mouths all of the 3 went out. There has been some other mild within the room now, one thousand times brighter than the night time-lighting fixtures, and in the time we have taken to mention this, it have been in all the drawers inside the nursery, searching out peter's shadow, rummaged the cloth wardrobe and grew to turn out to be every pocket inner out. It became not truely a mild; it made this mild by means of flashing about so short, but even as it came to relaxation for a 2d you noticed it become a fairy, not than your hand, but nevertheless growing. It grow to be a girl referred to as tinker bell exquisitely gowned in a skeleton leaf, lessen low and square, through which her decide may be visible to the best gain. She turned into slightly willing to embonpoint. [plump hourglass figure]

a second after the fairy's front the window changed into blown open by way of the respiratory of the little stars, and peter dropped in. He had carried tinker bell a part of the manner, and his hand become though messy with the fairy dust.

"tinker bell," he known as softly, after making sure that the kids had been asleep, "tink, in which are you?" she changed into in a jug for the immediate, and liking it extremely; she had by no means been in a jug before.

"oh, do come out of that jug, and tell me, do you recognize wherein they positioned my shadow?"

the maximum cute tinkle as of golden bells answered him. It is the fairy language. You regular kids can by no means listen it, but if you were to pay interest it you will recognize which you had heard it once in advance than. Tink said that the shadow became inside the large subject. She meant the chest of drawers, and peter jumped on the drawers, scattering their contents to the ground with both arms, as kings toss ha'pence to the gang. In a second he had recovered his shadow, and in his satisfaction he forgot that he had shut tinker bell up inside the drawer. If he concept the least bit, but i do now not recollect he ever concept, it become that he and his shadow, whilst delivered close to every one of a kind, could be a part of like drops of water, and when they did now not he become appalled. He tried to paste it on with soap from the bathroom, however that also failed. A shudder surpassed thru peter, and he sat at the ground and cried. His sobs woke wendy, and she or he sat up in mattress. She became no longer alarmed to peer a stranger crying at the nursery ground; she changed into best pleasantly interested.

"boy," she said with courtesy, "why are you crying?"

peter is probably exceeding well mannered additionally, having discovered out the grand manner at fairy ceremonies, and he rose and bowed to her superbly. She became plenty thrilled, and bowed noticeably to him from the mattress.

"what's your name?" he asked.

"wendy moira angela darling," she spoke back with some pleasure. "what's your name?"

"peter pan."

she turned into already positive that he want to be peter, but it did seem a tremendously short name.

"is that every one?"

"yes," he stated as an alternative sharply. He felt for the number one time that it was a shortish call.

"i am so sorry," stated wendy moira angela.

"it'd not depend," peter gulped. She asked in which he lived.

"2nd to the proper," stated peter, "and then right away on till morning."

"what a funny deal with!"

peter had a sinking. For the first time he felt that probable it turned into a humorous cope with.

"no, it is not," he stated.

"i suggest," wendy said well, remembering that she end up hostess, "is that what they placed on the letters?"

he wanted she had not stated letters.

"do not get any letters," he stated contemptuously.

"however your mom receives letters?"

"do not have a mom," he said. No longer handiest had he no mother, however he had now not the slightest preference to have one. He idea them very over-rated people. Wendy, however, felt right now that she became within the presence of a tragedy.

"o peter, no wonder you were crying," she said, and had been given far from mattress and ran to him.

"i wasn't crying about mothers," he said as an alternative indignantly. "i was crying due to the fact i cannot get my shadow to stick on. Except, i wasn't crying."

"it has come off?"

"sure."

then wendy noticed the shadow at the ground, searching so draggled, and she or he become frightfully sorry for peter. "how lousy!" she said, however she could not help smiling at the same time as she noticed that he had been in search of to stick it on with cleaning soap. How exactly like a boy! Fortuitously she knew without delay what to do. "it must be sewn on," she stated, only a touch patronisingly.

"what is sewn?" he asked.

"you are dreadfully ignorant."

"no, i'm now not."

but she turn out to be exulting in his lack of understanding. "i shall stitch it on for you, my little guy," she said, even though he modified into tall as herself, and he or she or he had been given out her housewife [sewing bag], and sewed the shadow directly to peter's foot.

"i daresay it'll hurt a little," she warned him.

"oh, i shan't cry," said peter, who became already of the opinion that he had in no manner cried in his lifestyles. And he clenched his tooth and did not cry, and soon his shadow became behaving well, despite the fact that nevertheless a bit creased.

"perhaps i must have ironed it," wendy stated thoughtfully, however peter, boylike, changed into detached to appearances, and he become now leaping about inside the wildest glee. Unluckily, he had already forgotten that he owed his bliss to wendy. He idea he had attached the shadow himself. "how clever i am!" he crowed rapturously, "oh, the cleverness of me!"

it's far humiliating to must confess that this conceit of peter grow to be certainly one of his maximum captivating tendencies. To position it with brutal frankness, there in no way become a cockier boy. But for the moment wendy modified into taken aback. "you conceit [braggart]," she exclaimed, with frightful sarcasm; "of course i did not anything!"

"you likely did a piece," peter stated carelessly, and persisted to dance.

"a bit!" she responded with hauteur [pride]; "if i'm little need i'm able to at the least withdraw," and she or he sprang inside the most dignified way into mattress and protected her face with the blankets. To result in her to appearance up he pretended to be going away, and whilst this failed he sat at the prevent of the mattress and tapped her lightly together with his foot. "wendy," he stated, "do not withdraw. I cannot help crowing, wendy, whilst i'm pleased with myself." still she might now not appearance up, although she changed into listening eagerly. "wendy," he continued, in a voice that no woman has ever but been able to face up to, "wendy, one girl is more use than twenty boys."

now wendy modified into each inch a female, despite the fact that there have been no longer very many inches, and she or he or he peeped out of the mattress-garments.

"do you in fact count on so, peter?"

"certain, i do."

"i suppose it is flawlessly candy of you," she declared, "and i'm able to get up once more," and he or she sat with him on the issue of the mattress. She additionally said she may give him a kiss if he favored, but peter did not recognize what she intended, and he held out his hand confidently.

"certainly what a kiss is?" she requested, aghast.

"i shall recognize even as you supply it to me," he responded stiffly, and no longer to hurt his feeling she gave him a thimble.

"now," said he, "shall i come up with a kiss?" and she or he replied with a moderate primness, "in case you please." she made herself as an alternative reasonably-priced with the aid of the usage of inclining her face closer to him, however he merely dropped an acorn button into her hand, so she slowly once more her face to wherein it were earlier than, and stated well that she may want to placed on his kiss at the chain round her neck. It was lucky that she did positioned it on that chain, for it became afterwards to store her life. Even as human beings in our set are delivered, it's miles everyday for them to ask every special's age, and so wendy, who constantly desired to do the ideal element, asked peter how vintage he come to be. It changed into now not without a doubt a glad question to ask him; it turned into like an examination paper that asks grammar, when what you want to be requested is kings of britain.

"i do now not recognise," he responded uneasily, "but i'm pretty more youthful." he truly knew no longer whatever approximately it, he had truly suspicions, however he stated at a project, "wendy, i ran away the day i used to be born."

wendy changed into quite amazed, however worried; and she indicated in the captivating drawing-room way, via a hint on her night time time-robe, that he may additionally want to sit nearer her.

"it end up because i heard mothers and fathers," he described in a low voice, "talking approximately what i used to be to be whilst i've emerge as someone." he changed into fairly agitated now. "i don't want ever to be a person," he said with ardour. "i want constantly to be a piece boy and to have a laugh. So i ran away to kensington gardens and lived a long long time maximum of the fairies."

she gave him a glance of the most severe admiration, and he idea it changed into due to the fact he had run away, however it become virtually because of the fact he knew fairies. Wendy had lived the form of domestic life that to realise fairies struck her as quite first-rate. She poured out questions on them, to his surprise, for they were rather a nuisance to him, entering into his way and so on, and certainly he every now and then needed to supply them a hiding [spanking]. Nonetheless, he favored them on the complete, and he instructed her about the start of fairies.

"you notice, wendy, while the first little one laughed for the number one time, its chuckle broke into 1000 quantities, and they all went skipping approximately, and that modified into the begin of fairies."

tedious communicate this, however being a stay-at-home she desired it.

"and so," he went on specific-naturedly, "there have to be one fairy for every boy and lady."

"should be? Isn't always there?"

"no. You spot kids understand such masses now, they quickly do not accept as true with in fairies, and each time a baby says, 'i don't bear in mind in fairies,' there is a fairy somewhere that falls down useless."

genuinely, he idea they had now talked sufficient approximately fairies, and it struck him that tinker bell turn out to be keeping very quiet. "i cannot assume wherein she has lengthy gone to," he said, growing, and he known as tink by the use of name. Wendy's heart went flutter with a unexpected thrill.

"peter," she cried, clutching him, "you do now not mean to tell me that there's a fairy in this room!"

"she turned into proper right here simply now," he said a touch impatiently. "you don't pay attention her, do you?" and they both listened.

"the high-quality sound i pay attention," said wendy, "is kind of a tinkle of bells."

"well, it's miles tink, that is the fairy language. I assume i concentrate her too."

the sound come from the chest of drawers, and peter made a merry face. No one may additionally need to ever appearance quite so merry as peter, and the most endearing of gurgles changed into his giggle. He had his first giggle nevertheless.

"wendy," he whispered gleefully, "i do consider i near her up in the drawer!"

he let awful tink out of the drawer, and she flew about the nursery screaming with fury. "you ought to now not say such things," peter retorted. "of direction i'm very sorry, however how have to i realize you have been within the drawer?"

wendy became no longer taking note of him. "o peter," she cried, "if she would possibly best stand nevertheless and permit me see her!"

"they rarely stand still," he stated, but for one 2d wendy noticed the romantic figure come to rest at the cuckoo clock. "o the lovely!" she cried, even though tink's face changed into nonetheless distorted with ardour.

"tink," said peter amiably, "this girl says she needs you had been her fairy."

tinker bell replied insolently.

"what does she say, peter?"

he had to translate. "she is not very polite. She says you're a first-rate [huge] unpleasant girl, and that she is my fairy."

he tried to argue with tink. "you apprehend you can't be my fairy, tink, due to the fact i am an gentleman and you're a female."

to this tink spoke back in those phrases, "you stupid ass," and disappeared into the rest room. "she is quite a commonplace fairy," peter defined apologetically, "she is referred to as tinker bell due to the fact she mends the pots and kettles [tinker = tin worker]." [similar to "cinder" plus "elle" to get cinderella]

they have been collectively in the armchair with the aid of way of this time, and wendy plied him with more questions.

"if you do not stay in kensington gardens now—"

"every now and then i do despite the fact that."

"however wherein do you stay usually now?"

"with the lost boys."

"who're they?"

"they'll be the youngsters who fall out in their perambulators while the nurse is looking the opposite manner. If they're not claimed in seven days they may be sent a long way away to the neverland to defray charges. I'm captain."

"what fun it have to be!"

"sure," said foxy peter, "but we're instead lonely. You notice we have no girl companionship."

"are none of the others ladies?"

"oh, no; women, , are a good buy too smart to fall out of their prams."

this flattered wendy immensely. "i suppose," she stated, "it's miles flawlessly adorable the manner you talk about ladies; john there clearly despises us."

for reply peter rose and kicked john away from bed, blankets and all; one kick. This appeared to wendy instead ahead for a primary meeting, and she told him with spirit that he became not captain in her house. But, john persevered to sleep so placidly on the floor that she allowed him to live there. "and i understand you alleged to be type," she said, relenting, "so that you can also deliver me a kiss."

for the moment she had forgotten his lack of know-how about kisses. "i concept you will need it decrease lower back," he stated a bit bitterly, and presented to go back her the thimble.

"oh luxurious," stated the first rate wendy, "i do now not mean a kiss, i suggest a thimble."

"what is that?"

"it is like this." she kissed him.

"humorous!" stated peter gravely. "now shall i come up with a thimble?"

"if you want to," stated wendy, preserving her head erect this time. Peter thimbled her, and nearly right away she screeched. "what's it, wendy?"

"it become precisely as even though someone had been pulling my hair."

"that should have been tink. I in no way knew her so naughty earlier than."

and without a doubt tink changed into darting about yet again, the use of offensive language.

"she says she will do this to you, wendy, whenever i offer you with a thimble."

"but why?"

"why, tink?"

all over again tink responded, "you stupid ass." peter could not apprehend why, but wendy understood, and she grow to be in reality barely dissatisfied whilst he admitted that he came to the nursery window no longer to see her but to take note of memories.

"you notice, i do not know any recollections. Not one of the misplaced boys knows any tales."

"how flawlessly awful," wendy said.

"do you recognize," peter requested "why swallows construct within the eaves of homes? It is to pay attention to the memories. O wendy, your mother changed into telling you this kind of cute tale."

"which story emerge as it?"

"about the prince who could not discover the female who wore the glass slipper."

"peter," said wendy excitedly, "that changed into cinderella, and he positioned her, and that they lived fortuitously ever after."

peter changed into so glad that he rose from the floor, in which they had been sitting, and moved quickly to the window.

"where are you going?" she cried with misgiving.

"to inform the opposite boys."

"don't move peter," she entreated, "i recognize such hundreds of recollections."

the ones had been her unique phrases, so there can be no denying that it was she who first tempted him. He got here lower back, and there has been a greedy look in his eyes now which ought to have alarmed her, but did not.

"oh, the tales i may also want to inform to the lads!" she cried, after which peter gripped her and commenced to attract her within the course of the window.

"permit me pass!" she ordered him.

"wendy, do consist of me and tell the alternative boys."

of route she changed into very pleased to be requested, however she said, "oh expensive, i can't. Recall mummy! Except, i can't fly."

"i'm able to teach you."

"oh, how lovable to fly."

"i will train you a way to bounce at the wind's returned, and then away we go."

"oo!" she exclaimed rapturously.

"wendy, wendy, while you're slumbering to your stupid bed you is probably flying approximately with me announcing funny matters to the celebs."

"oo!"

"and, wendy, there are mermaids."

"mermaids! With tails?"

"such lengthy tails."

"oh," cried wendy, "to look a mermaid!"

he had emerge as frightfully foxy. "wendy," he stated, "how we have to all admire you."

she turned into wriggling her body in misery. It was quite as though she were searching for to stay on the nursery floor. But he had no pity for her.

"wendy," he said, the sly one, "you could tuck us in at night time."

"oo!"

"none oldsters has ever been tucked in at night."

"oo," and her fingers went out to him.

"and you may darn our garments, and make pockets for us. None folks has any wallet."

how ought to she withstand. "of direction it's miles relatively fascinating!" she cried. "peter, should you teach john and michael to fly too?"

"if you like," he stated indifferently, and she or he or he ran to john and michael and shook them. "awaken," she cried, "peter pan has come and he is to teach us to fly."

john rubbed his eyes. "then i shall upward push up," he stated. Of course he changed into on the floor already. "hallo," he said, "i am up!"

michael turned into up via the use of this time moreover, looking as sharp as a knife with six blades and a noticed, however peter abruptly signed silence. Their faces assumed the awful craftiness of kids listening for sounds from the grown-up global. All changed into as nevertheless as salt. Then the entirety grow to be right. No, prevent! The whole thing changed into wrong. Nana, who have been barking distressfully all the nighttime, become quiet now. It come to be her silence that they had heard.

"out with the light! Conceal! Brief!" cried john, taking command for the fine time at some point of the whole journey. And for this reason even as liza entered, retaining nana, the nursery appeared quite its old self, very dark, and you will have sworn you heard its three depraved inmates respiratory angelically as they slept. They have been surely doing it artfully from in the back of the window curtains. Liza turned into in a awful temper, for she become blending the christmas puddings inside the kitchen, and have been drawn from them, with a raisin nevertheless on her cheek, thru nana's absurd suspicions. She notion the first-rate way of having a chunk quiet became to take nana to the nursery for a moment, however in custody of course.

"there, you suspicious brute," she said, not sorry that nana have become in shame. "they're perfectly safe, aren't they? Each one of the little angels slumbering in mattress. Be aware of their slight respiration."

right here michael, encouraged through way of his achievement, breathed so loudly that they were nearly detected. Nana knew that sort of respiratory, and he or she or he tried to pull herself out of liza's clutches. However liza become dense. "no extra of it, nana," she stated sternly, pulling her out of the room. "i provide you with a warning if bark over again i shall go without delay for master and missus and produce them domestic from the party, and then, oh, won't grasp whip you, actually."

she tied the unhappy dog up once more, but do you observed nana ceased to bark? Supply grasp and missus domestic from the birthday celebration! Why, that became just what she desired. Do you consider you studied she cared whether or no longer she changed into whipped so long as her charges have been comfy? Sadly liza lower again to her puddings, and nana, seeing that no assist could come from her, strained and strained on the chain till at last she broke it. In some other 2nd she had burst into the dining-room of 27 and flung up her paws to heaven, her most expressive manner of making a communique. Mr. And mrs. Darling knew right now that some component terrible have become taking place of their nursery, and without a excellent-bye to their hostess they rushed into the road. However it became now ten minutes considering that three scoundrels were respiration behind the curtains, and peter pan can do a extremely good deal in ten mins. We now move returned to the nursery.

"it is all right," john announced, emerging from his hiding-region. "i say, peter, are you able to clearly fly?"

as opposed to troubling to answer him peter flew across the room, taking the mantelpiece at the way.

"how topping!" stated john and michael.

"how candy!" cried wendy.

"sure, i'm sweet, oh, i'm sweet!" said peter, forgetting his manners once more. It seemed delightfully clean, and that they tried it first from the floor after which from the beds, however they constantly went down in area of up.

"i say, how do you do it?" requested john, rubbing his knee. He became pretty a realistic boy.

"you simply count on cute incredible mind," peter defined, "and that they elevate you up within the air."

he confirmed them all over again.

"you're so nippy at it," john stated, "couldn't you do it very slowly as quickly as?"

peter did it each slowly and rapid. "i've were given it now, wendy!" cried john, but fast he decided he had not. No longer one in every of them may want to fly an inch, even though even michael become in phrases of two syllables, and peter did no longer realise a from z. Of route peter have been trifling with them, for nobody can fly except the fairy dust has been blown on him. Happily, as we've mentioned, one in each of his arms changed into messy with it, and he blew some on every of them, with the maximum fantastic results.

"now surely wiggle your shoulders this way," he stated, "and let cross."

they had been all on their beds, and gallant michael permit circulate first. He did now not quite suggest to permit flow, however he did it, and proper now he come to be borne for the duration of the room.

"i flewed!" he screamed whilst though in mid-air. John permit pass and met wendy close to the bathroom.

"oh, lovable!"

"oh, ripping!"

"take a look at me!"

"take a look at me!"

"observe me!"

they have been now not almost so stylish as peter, they could not help kicking a bit, however their heads had been bobbing in competition to the ceiling, and there is nearly nothing so scrumptious as that. Peter gave wendy a hand at the beginning, but had to desist, tink changed into so angry. Up and down they went, and round and spherical. Heavenly become wendy's phrase.

"i say," cried john, "why should now not anyone exit?"

of direction it become to this that peter had been luring them. Michael changed into organized: he desired to look how long it took him to do a thousand million miles. However wendy hesitated.

"mermaids!" stated peter once more.

"oo!"

"and there are pirates."

"pirates," cried john, seizing his sunday hat, "permit us to pass right away."

it emerge as without a doubt at this moment that mr. And mrs. Darling moved quick with nana out of 27. They bumped into the center of the road to appearance up at the nursery window; and, certain, it grow to be nevertheless close, however the room become ablaze with slight, and most heart-gripping sight of all, they'll see in shadow at the curtain three little figures in night time clothing circling round and spherical, not at the ground however in the air. Not 3 figures, four! In a tremble they opened the road door. Mr. Darling might have rushed upstairs, however mrs. Darling signed him to head softly. She even attempted to make her coronary heart pass softly. Will they attain the nursery in time? If so, how excellent for them, and we shall all breathe a sigh of comfort, however there might be no story. As an alternative, if they may be not in time, i solemnly promise that it'll all come proper in the long run. They could have reached the nursery in time had it now not been that the little stars have been watching them. Over again the stars blew the window open, and that smallest superstar of all called out:

"cave, peter!"

then peter knew that there has been no longer a 2d to lose. "come," he cried imperiously, and soared out proper away into the night time, discovered through john and michael and wendy. Mr. And mrs. Darling and nana rushed into the nursery too past due. The birds were flown.

Chapter

4

the flight

"second to the proper, and right away on until morning."

that, peter had recommended wendy, was the manner to the neverland; but even birds, wearing maps and consulting them at windy corners, could not have sighted it with the ones instructions. Peter, you notice, simply stated a few aspect that got here into his head. Within the beginning his partners depended on him implicitly, and so first-rate had been the delights of flying that they wasted time circling round church spires or any other tall gadgets on the manner that took their fancy. John and michael raced, michael getting a begin. They recalled with contempt that no longer goodbye ago they'd thought themselves quality fellows for being able to fly spherical a room. Now not lengthy in the past. But how lengthy within the past? They had been flying over the sea in advance than this concept began to disturb wendy critically. John idea it changed into their 2nd sea and their third night time. From time to time it have become darkish and on occasion slight, and now they had been very cold and again too warm. Did they really experience hungry at times, or had been they sincerely pretending, due to the fact peter had this sort of jolly new way of feeding them? His manner have become to pursue birds who had meals in their mouths suitable for humans and take keep of it from them; then the birds could follow and snatch it again; and they would all pass chasing every different gaily for miles, parting at remaining with mutual expressions of suitable-will. However wendy located with mild trouble that peter did no longer seem to know that this become as an alternative an ordinary way of getting your bread and butter, nor even that there are special ways. Surely they did now not fake to be sleepy, they were sleepy; and that become a hazard, for the instant they popped off, down they fell. The lousy component emerge as that peter concept this humorous.

"there he goes once more!" he could cry gleefully, as michael all of sudden dropped like a stone.

"hold him, keep him!" cried wendy, searching with horror at the merciless sea far beneath. Eventually peter might dive via the air, and trap michael simply in advance than he need to strike the ocean, and it emerge as lovable the manner he did it; however he normally waited till the remaining second, and you felt it became his cleverness that fascinated him and now not the saving of human lifestyles. Also he became fond of range, and the game that engrossed him one second could all of sudden forestall to have interaction him, so there has been continually the possibility that the following time you fell he could let you pass. He ought to sleep in the air without falling, by way of the use of simply mendacity on his again and floating, but this emerge as, partly as a minimum, because he became so light that if you got at the back of him and blew he went quicker.

"do be greater well mannered to him," wendy whispered to john, once they were playing "follow my chief."

"then inform him to forestall displaying off," stated john. Whilst playing observe my chief, peter may fly near the water and phone each shark's tail in passing, simply as in the road you can run your finger along an iron railing. They could not take a look at him in this with an awful lot success, so likely it changed into as an opportunity like showing off, in particular as he saved searching in the returned of to peer how many tails they left out.

"you need to be terrific to him," wendy inspired on her brothers. "what could we do if he had been to go away us!"

"we need to bypass returned," michael stated.

"how can also want to we ever discover our manner again without him?"

"well, then, we may also want to move on," stated john.

"that is the awful issue, john. We need to want to move on, for we do no longer recognise a manner to prevent."

this become actual, peter had forgotten to show them the way to forestall. John said that if the worst came to the worst, all they had to do changed into to go without delay on, for the sector was round, and so in time they must come once more to their own window.

"and who is to get meals for us, john?"

"i nipped a chunk out of that eagle's mouth pretty neatly, wendy."

"after the twentieth attempt," wendy reminded him. "and regardless of the truth that we've turn out to be accurate a selecting up meals, see how we bump towards clouds and matters if he is not near to present us a hand."

certainly they have been continuously bumping. They could now fly strongly, even though they nevertheless kicked far an excessive amount of; but inside the occasion that they observed a cloud in the the front of them, the greater they tried to keep away from it, the extra sincerely did they come upon it. If nana had been with them, she ought to have had a bandage spherical michael's forehead via using this time. Peter changed into now not with them for the immediate, and they felt as an opportunity lonely up there through themselves. He ought to move a lot faster than they that he could suddenly shoot out of sight, to have some adventure wherein that that they had no percentage. He could come down guffawing over something fearfully funny he were announcing to a celebrity, but he had already forgotten what it turn out to be, or he could offer you with mermaid scales though sticking to him, and but no longer be able to say for sure what have been occurring. It modified into certainly alternatively stressful to kids who had in no way visible a mermaid.

"and if he forgets them so quick," wendy argued, "how can we assume that he is going to go on remembering us?"

without a doubt, sometimes while he again he did now not keep in mind them, as a minimum now not well. Wendy modified into superb of it. She observed reputation come into his eyes as he modified into about to skip them the time of day and move on; as soon as even she had to name him by manner of name.

"i am wendy," she stated agitatedly. He became very sorry. "i say, wendy," he whispered to her, "constantly if you see me forgetting you, virtually preserve on pronouncing 'i'm wendy,' and then i'll consider."

of direction this was alternatively unsatisfactory. However, to make amends he showed them a manner to lie out flat on a strong wind that modified into going their manner, and this become such a pleasant exchange that they attempted it numerous times and determined that they might sleep because of this with protection. Indeed they might have slept longer, however peter worn-out rapid of sleeping, and shortly he might cry in his captain voice, "we get off here." so with occasional tiffs, but at the entire rollicking, they drew near the neverland; for after many moons they did attain it, and, what's extra, they had been going quite right away all of the time, not possibly loads as a consequence of the steering of peter or tink as because the island was searching out them. It is most effective because of this that everyone also can sight the ones magic seashores.

"there it is," stated peter lightly.

"wherein, in which?"

"in which all of the arrows are pointing."

in reality a million golden arrows were pointing it out to the kids, all directed with the aid of way in their buddy the sun, who desired them to make sure in their way in advance than leaving them for the night time. Wendy and john and michael stood on tip-toe in the air to get their first sight of the island. Strange to mention, all of them recognized it straight away, and till fear fell upon them they hailed it, not as something lengthy dreamt of and seen at final, but as a acquainted buddy to whom they were returning home for the vacations.

"john, there may be the lagoon."

"wendy, observe the turtles burying their eggs in the sand."

"i say, john, i see your flamingo with the broken leg!"

"appearance, michael, there may be your cave!"

"john, what is that inside the brushwood?"

"it's a wolf in conjunction with her whelps. Wendy, i do accept as true with it is your little whelp!"

"there's my boat, john, together along with her aspects range in!"

"no, it is not. Why, we burned your boat."

"this is her, at any price. I say, john, i see the smoke of the redskin camp!"

"where? Display me, and i can tell you with the useful resource of the manner smoke curls whether or not they're at the warfare-direction."

"there, simply across the mysterious river."

"i see now. Certain, they're at the struggle-direction right enough."

peter changed into a little irritated with them for knowing loads, but if he favored to lord it over them his triumph have become accessible, for have i no longer told you that anon worry fell upon them? It got here because the arrows went, leaving the island in gloom. Within the vintage days at domestic the neverland had constantly began to appearance a piece dark and dangerous with the aid of bedtime. Then unexplored patches arose in it and unfold, black shadows moved approximately in them, the roar of the beasts of prey was quite specific now, and in particular, you out of place the knowledge which you may win. You were quite glad that the night time-lights had been on. You even liked nana to say that this end up just the mantelpiece over proper right here, and that the neverland was all make-trust. Of path the neverland were make-agree with inside the ones days, however it modified into real now, and there have been no night time-lights, and it have become getting darker every second, and wherein changed into nana? They were flying aside, but they huddled near peter now. His careless manner had lengthy long gone at last, his eyes had been sparkling, and a tingle went thru them each time they touched his frame. They were now over the fearsome island, flying so low that sometimes a tree grazed their ft. Now not whatever horrid become seen inside the air, but their development had turn out to be slow and laboured, exactly as if they have been pushing their manner thru destructive forces. From time to time they hung in the air until peter had crushed on it along with his fists.

"they do not want us to land," he defined.

"who are they?" wendy whispered, shuddering. But he couldn't or ought to not say. Tinker bell had been asleep on his shoulder, but now he woke up her and sent her on in front. Every so often he poised himself within the air, listening carefully, along along with his hand to his ear, and once more he could stare down with eyes so amazing that they appeared to bore holes to earth. Having finished these things, he went on once more. His braveness grow to be almost appalling. "would possibly you like an journey now," he said casually to john, "or might you need to have your tea first?"

wendy stated "tea first" rapid, and michael pressed her hand in gratitude, but the braver john hesitated.

"what shape of adventure?" he asked carefully.

"there's a pirate asleep inside the pampas definitely below us," peter informed him. "in case you want, we are going to skip down and kill him."

"i do no longer see him," john stated after an prolonged pause.

"i do."

"anticipate," john stated, a piece huskily, "he have been to wake up."

peter spoke indignantly. "you do now not suppose i'd kill him while he end up drowsing! I'd wake him first, after which kill him. This is the manner i continually do."

"i say! Do you kill many?"

"lots."

john said "how ripping," but determined to have tea first. He requested if there were many pirates on the island simply now, and peter stated he had in no way seemed such a variety of.

"who is captain now?"

"hook," replied peter, and his face have turn out to be very stern as he said that hated word.

"jas. Hook?"

"ay."

then certainly michael started out to cry, or maybe john may additionally need to talk in gulps best, for they knew hook's reputation.

"he changed into blackbeard's bo'sun," john whispered huskily. "he is the worst of all of them. He's the handiest man of whom barbecue modified into afraid."

"it actually is him," said peter.

"what's he like? Is he big?"

"he is not so large as he become."

"how do you mean?"

"i reduce off a piece of him."

"you!"

"yes, me," said peter sharply.

"i wasn't meaning to be disrespectful."

"oh, all right."

"however, i say, what bit?"

"his proper hand."

"then he can not combat now?"

"oh, can't he absolutely!"

"left-hander?"

"he has an iron hook as opposed to a proper hand, and he claws with it."

"claws!"

"i say, john," said peter.

"positive."

"say, 'ay, ay, sir.'"

"ay, ay, sir."

"there is one thing," peter persisted, "that each boy who serves under me has to promise, and so need to you."

john paled.

"it's far this, if we meet hook in open combat, you need to depart him to me."

"i promise," john said loyally. For the moment they have been feeling much less eerie, because tink become flying with them, and in her mild they could distinguish each other. Lamentably she could not fly so slowly as they, and so she needed to cross spherical and spherical them in a circle in which they moved as in a halo. Wendy quite favored it, till peter noted the drawbacks.

"she tells me," he said, "that the pirates sighted us before the darkness came, and got prolonged tom out."

"the massive gun?"

"yes. And of course they need to see her mild, and within the event that they bet we're close to it they are sure to allow fly."

"wendy!"

"john!"

"michael!"

"tell her to go away right now, peter," the three cried simultaneously, however he refused.

"she thinks we've misplaced the manner," he spoke back stiffly, "and she or he is as an alternative worried. You do not assume i might deliver her away all with the aid of the use of herself at the same time as she is irritating!"

for a moment the circle of moderate become broken, and something gave peter a loving little pinch.

"then tell her," wendy begged, "to place out her mild."

"she cannot placed it out. That is about the satisfactory thing fairies cannot do. It simply goes out of itself at the same time as she falls asleep, equal due to the fact the stars."

"then inform her to sleep right away," john almost ordered.

"she can't sleep besides when she's sleepy. It's miles the most effective different issue fairies cannot do."

"seems to me," growled john, "these are the best things nicely really worth doing."

here he were given a pinch, but now not a loving one.

"if handiest one folks had a pocket," peter said, "we need to supply her in it." however, that they had prompt on this type of hurry that there was no longer a pocket a few of the four of them. He had a satisfied concept. John's hat! Tink agreed to excursion with the aid of the usage of hat if it changed into carried within the hand. John carried it, even though she had hoped to be carried via peter. Presently wendy took the hat, because john said it struck in the direction of his knee as he flew; and this, as we will see, caused mischief, for tinker bell hated to be beneath an responsibility to wendy. Inside the black topper the mild was virtually hidden, and that they flew on in silence. It became the stillest silence they'd ever acknowledged, damaged as soon as by way of using lapping, which peter defined modified into the wild beasts consuming at the ford, and over again by using the usage of a rasping sound that might have been the branches of wood rubbing collectively, but he stated it changed into the redskins sprucing their knives. Even these noises ceased. To michael the loneliness have become dreadful. "if exceptional something would possibly make a valid!" he cried. As although in solution to his request, the air became lease through the usage of the maximum superb crash he had ever heard. The pirates had fired prolonged tom at them. The roar of it echoed through the mountains, and the echoes regarded to cry savagely, "in that are they, in which might be they, where are they?"

as a result sharply did the terrified three analyze the distinction between an island of make-believe and the identical island come authentic. While at very last the heavens were consistent once more, john and michael located themselves on my own within the darkness. John became treading the air mechanically, and michael without understanding a manner to glide have become floating.

"are you shot?" john whispered tremulously.

"i have never attempted [myself out] but," michael whispered back. We understand now that no one had been hit. Peter, but, have been carried via way of the wind of the shot a long way out to sea, even as wendy become blown upwards without a companion however tinker bell. It'd had been properly for wendy if at that second she had dropped the hat. I don't know whether or not the idea came suddenly to tink, or whether she had planned it on the way, however she proper away popped out of the hat and started out out to lure wendy to her destruction. Tink have become now not all awful; or, as a substitute, she become all horrific definitely now, but, alternatively, now and again she was all particular. Fairies want to be one component or the opposite, because being so small they unfortunately have room for one feeling best at a time. They are, but, allowed to exchange, simplest it need to be a whole alternate. At present she have become entire of jealousy of wendy. What she stated in her cute tinkle wendy could not of direction recognize, and that i don't forget some of it was horrible phrases, however it sounded kind, and she or he flew once more and ahead, it appears that obviously which means "study me, and all can be nicely."

what else have to awful wendy do? She known as to peter and john and michael, and got only mocking echoes in respond. She did no longer but recognise that tink hated her with the fierce hatred of a very girl. And so, bewildered, and now stunning in her flight, she determined tink to her doom.

Chapter

5

the island come authentic

feeling that peter was on his manner again, the neverland had yet again woke into existence. We need to use the pluperfect and say woke up, however woke is higher and have become continuously used by peter. In his absence topics are commonly quiet at the island. The fairies take an hour longer in the morning, the beasts attend to their younger, the redskins feed closely for 6 days and nights, and whilst pirates and misplaced boys meet they merely bite their thumbs at each other. However with the coming of peter, who hates lethargy, they're below way again: if you put your ear to the ground now, you'll pay attention the whole island seething with existence. In this nighttime the leader forces of the island had been disposed as follows. The misplaced boys were out looking for peter, the pirates had been out looking for the misplaced boys, the redskins were out searching out the pirates, and the beasts have been out seeking out the redskins. They were going spherical and spherical the island, however they did no longer meet due to the fact all had been going at the identical fee. All desired blood besides the boys, who preferred it maximum normally, however to-night time were out to greet their captain. The lads on the island variety, of path, in numbers, according as they get killed and so forth; and after they look like growing up, that's in the direction of the regulations, peter thins them out; but presently there were six of them, counting the twins as . Let us pretend to lie here the numerous sugar-cane and watch them as they steal by way of manner of in unmarried file, every collectively with his hand on his dagger. They may be forbidden by means of using peter to look in the least like him, and that they put on the skins of the bears slain by using themselves, wherein they're so round and bushy that after they fall they roll. They have therefore come to be very superb-footed. The primary to pass is tootles, not the least courageous however the most unlucky of all that gallant band. He were in fewer adventures than any of them, due to the fact the huge subjects constantly took place sincerely while he had stepped round the corner; all could be quiet, he might take the opportunity of going off to accumulate some sticks for firewood, and then at the same time as he returned the others could be sweeping up the blood. This unwell luck had given a slight despair to his countenance, but as opposed to souring his nature had sweetened it, in order that he became quite the humblest of the boys. Terrible kind tootles, there's threat within the air a good way to-night time. Take care lest an adventure is now provided you, which, if universal, will plunge you in internal maximum woe. Tootles, the fairy tink, who is bent on mischief this night time is seeking out a tool [for doing her mischief], and she or he thinks you're the most without problem tricked of the men. 'ware tinker bell. Would possibly that he must pay attention us, however we are not surely on the island, and he passes via, biting his knuckles. Subsequent comes nibs, the gay and debonair, found via slightly, who cuts whistles out of the timber and dances ecstatically to his very very own tunes. Barely is the most conceited of the lads. He thinks he recalls the instances earlier than he modified into misplaced, with their manners and customs, and this has given his nose an offensive tilt. Curly is fourth; he's a pickle, [a person who gets in pickles-predicaments] and so often has he had to supply up his character while peter said sternly, "stand forth the most effective who did this issue," that now at the command he stands forth automatically whether or not he has performed it or not. Last come the twins, who cannot be described due to the truth we must make sure to be describing the incorrect one. Peter never quite knew what twins were, and his band have been now not allowed to recognise some thing he did not understand, so those had been usually vague approximately themselves, and did their first-rate to provide pride through preserving near collectively in an apologetic form of way. The men vanish inside the gloom, and after a pause, but now not a long pause, for matters skip right away on the island, come the pirates on their track. We pay interest them earlier than they're visible, and it is always the identical dreadful song:

"avast belay, yo ho, heave to,

a-pirating we cross,

and if we are parted via a shot

we're sure to satisfy beneath!"

a greater villainous-searching lot in no manner hung in a row on execution dock. Right here, a touch earlier, ever and once more together along with his head to the ground listening, his exceptional arms naked, portions of 8 in his ears as embellishes, is the handsome italian cecco, who lessen his call in letters of blood on the decrease back of the governor of the prison at gao. That vast black behind him has had many names given that he dropped the one with which dusky mothers despite the fact that terrify their kids on the banks of the guadjo-mo. Right here is invoice jukes, every inch of him tattooed, the same invoice jukes who have been given six dozen on the walrus from flint in advance than he could drop the bag of moidores [portuguese gold pieces]; and cookson, said to be black murphy's brother (however this was never proved), and gentleman starkey, as soon as an bring in a public school and despite the fact that dainty in his methods of killing; and skylights (morgan's skylights); and the irish bo'solar smee, an oddly genial man who stabbed, so to speak, without offence, and have become the quality non-conformist in hook's group; and noodler, whose fingers were constant on backwards; and robt. Mullins and alf mason and masses of every other ruffian prolonged seemed and feared at the spanish fundamental. Within the midst of them, the blackest and largest in that darkish putting, reclined james hook, or as he wrote himself, jas. Hook, of whom it's far said he became the best man that the ocean-put together dinner feared. He lay at his ease in a tough chariot drawn and propelled through his men, and in area of a proper hand he had the iron hook with which ever and anon he recommended them to growth their pace. As dogs this horrible guy treated and addressed them, and as puppies they obeyed him. In man or woman he changed into cadaverous [dead looking] and blackavized [dark faced], and his hair changed into carrying lengthy curls, which at a chunk distance appeared like black candles, and gave a singularly threatening expression to his handsome countenance. His eyes had been of the blue of the neglect-me-no longer, and of a profound depression, keep while he become plunging his hook into you, at which time purple spots appeared in them and lit them up horribly. In way, some issue of the grand seigneur nevertheless clung to him, in order that he even ripped you up with an air, and i've been suggested that he become a raconteur [storyteller] of reputation. He changed into by no means extra sinister than when he turned into maximum polite, which is probably the truest test of breeding; and the splendor of his diction, even though he became swearing, no tons much less than the difference of his demeanour, showed him considered one of a unique solid from his organization. A person of indomitable courage, it turn out to be said that the best element he shied at have become the sight of his very own blood, which become thick and of an unusual colour. In dress he actually aped the attire related to the call of charles ii, having heard it said in some earlier period of his career that he bore a peculiar resemblance to the ill-fated stuarts; and in his mouth he had a holder of his personal contrivance which enabled him to smoke cigars proper now. However definitely the grimmest part of him turn out to be his iron claw. Allow us to now kill a pirate, to expose hook's approach. Skylights will do. As they pass, skylights lurches clumsily towards him, ruffling his lace collar; the hook shoots forth, there's a tearing sound and one screech, then the frame is kicked apart, and the pirates skip on. He has now not even taken the cigars from his mouth. Such is the terrible man in opposition to whom peter pan is pitted. With a view to win? At the route of the pirates, stealing noiselessly down the struggle-course, which isn't always seen to inexperienced eyes, come the redskins, each one in all them collectively with his eyes peeled. They bring tomahawks and knives, and their naked our bodies gleam with paint and oil. Strung around them are scalps, of boys similarly to of pirates, for these are the piccaninny tribe, and not to be harassed with the softer-hearted delawares or the hurons. In the van, on all fours, is brilliant big little panther, a courageous of such a lot of scalps that in his present position they rather impede his improvement. Citing the rear, the area of finest risk, comes tiger lily, proudly erect, a princess in her very very own right. She is the maximum stunning of dusky dianas [diana = goddess of the woods] and the belle of the piccaninnies, coquettish [flirting], bloodless and amorous [loving] via turns; there isn't always a brave who may now not have the wayward problem to spouse, but she staves off the altar with a hatchet. Test how they bypass over fallen twigs with out making the slightest noise. The only sound to be heard is their pretty heavy respiratory. The reality is that they may be all a touch fats just now after the heavy gorging, but in time they'll work this off. For the immediate, but, it constitutes their leader risk. The redskins disappear as they have got come like shadows, and soon their location is taken through the beasts, a tremendous and motley procession: lions, tigers, bears, and the innumerable smaller savage matters that flee from them, for each kind of beast, and, more specially, all the guy-eaters, stay cheek with the resource of jowl at the favoured island. Their tongues are hanging out, they're hungry to-night time. After they have passed, comes the ultimate figure of all, a big crocodile. We will see for whom she is looking currently. The crocodile passes, but fast the boys appear once more, for the procession want to hold indefinitely till one of the occasions stops or changes its tempo. Then quick they'll be on pinnacle of every distinctive. All are retaining a sharp appearance-out in the the front, however none suspects that the risk may be creeping up from within the again of. This indicates how actual the island turn out to be. The number one to fall out of the shifting circle become the men. They flung themselves down on the sward [turf], near their underground domestic.

"i do want peter could come again," every surely considered one of them said nervously, even though in top and although greater in breadth they had been all big than their captain.

"i'm the handiest one that isn't terrified of the pirates," barely stated, inside the tone that avoided his being a preferred favored; however possibly a few distant sound disturbed him, for he introduced swiftly, "but i desire he would possibly come again, and inform us whether or not he has heard something extra approximately cinderella."

they talked of cinderella, and tootles come to be assured that his mom have to had been just like her. It modified into high-quality in peter's absence that they could speak of mothers, the priority being forbidden through him as silly.

"all i don't forget approximately my mom," nibs told them, "is that she often stated to my father, 'oh, how i want i had a cheque-e-book of my personal!' i do now not recognize what a cheque-ebook is, however i need to genuinely love to provide my mother one."

at the same time as they talked they heard sound. You or i, not being wild matters of the woods, might have heard not anything, but they heard it, and it was the grim music:

"yo ho, yo ho, the pirate life,

the flag o' cranium and bones,

a merry hour, a hempen rope,

and hello for davy jones."

immediately the lost boys—but wherein are they? They're no longer there. Rabbits could not have disappeared greater speedy. I will inform you where they're. Except nibs, who has darted away to reconnoitre [look around], they're already in their home under the ground, a completely first-class residence of which we shall see a good deal presently. However how have they reached it? For there can be no the front to be seen, no longer plenty as a massive stone, which if rolled away, might reveal the mouth of a cave. Appearance intently, however, and you can observe that there are here seven huge bushes, each with a hole in its hollow trunk as huge as a boy. The ones are the seven entrances to the residence under the ground, for which hook has been looking in useless the ones many moons. Will he find it this night? As the pirates superior, the short eye of starkey sighted nibs disappearing through the timber, and at once his pistol flashed out. But an iron claw gripped his shoulder.

"captain, allow move!" he cried, writhing. Now for the primary time we listen the voice of hook. It become a black voice. "positioned once more that pistol first," it said threateningly.

"it changed into one of these boys you hate. I may want to have shot him useless."

"ay, and the sound should have brought tiger lily's redskins upon us. Do you need to lose your scalp?"

"shall i after him, captain," requested pathetic smee, "and tickle him with johnny corkscrew?" smee had first-class names for the entirety, and his cutlass end up johnny corkscrew, because he wiggled it in the wound. One need to point out many cute traits in smee. For example, after killing, it was his spectacles he wiped rather than his weapon.

"johnny's a silent fellow," he reminded hook.

"now not now, smee," hook stated darkly. "he is handiest one, and i want to mischief all of the seven. Scatter and look for them."

the pirates disappeared among the bushes, and in a 2nd their captain and smee were by myself. Hook heaved a heavy sigh, and that i realise not why it become, perhaps it became due to the tender beauty of the nighttime, but there got here over him a desire to confide to his straightforward bo'sun the tale of his lifestyles. He spoke lengthy and earnestly, however what it become all about smee, who become as a substitute stupid, did not recognize within the least. Anon [later] he caught the word peter.

"most of all," hook become saying passionately, "i want their captain, peter pan. 'twas he reduce off my arm." he brandished the hook threateningly. "i've waited prolonged to shake his hand with this. Oh, i will tear him!"

"and yet," stated smee, "i've often heard you assert that hook became well worth a rating of fingers, for combing the hair and different homely uses."

"ay," the captain spoke back, "if i used to be a mom i'd pray to have my children born with this in preference to that," and he cast a glance of pride upon his iron hand and sincerely one of scorn upon the other. As an alternative he frowned.

"peter flung my arm," he stated, wincing, "to a crocodile that came about to be passing through."

"i've often," stated smee, "determined your weird dread of crocodiles."

"now not of crocodiles," hook corrected him, "but of that one crocodile." he lowered his voice. "it favored my arm lots, smee, that it has followed me ever considering, from sea to sea and from land to land, licking its lips for the rest of me."

"in a way," said smee, "it's far kind of a reward."

"i need no such compliments," hook barked petulantly. "i need peter pan, who first gave the brute its flavor for me."

he sat down on a huge mushroom, and now there has been a quiver in his voice. "smee," he said huskily, "that crocodile should have had me earlier than this, however by way of a lucky risk it swallowed a clock which goes tick tick inner it, and so earlier than it may attain me i pay attention the tick and bolt." he laughed, however in a hollow manner.

"a few day," stated smee, "the clock will run down, after which he is going to get you."

hook wetted his dry lips. "ay," he said, "it absolutely is the concern that haunts me."

for the motive that sitting down he had felt interestingly warmth. "smee," he stated, "this seat is heat." he jumped up. "odds bobs, hammer and tongs i'm burning."

they examined the mushroom, which become of a size and solidity unknown at the mainland; they tried to drag it up, and it came away immediately of their hands, for it had no root. Stranger nonetheless, smoke started straight away to ascend. The pirates looked at each distinctive. "a chimney!" they both exclaimed. They'd definitely discovered the chimney of the house underneath the ground. It grow to be the custom of the lads to stop it with a mushroom while enemies were within the neighbourhood. Now not simplest smoke got here out of it. There came also children's voices, for so secure did the boys sense in their hiding-region that they have got been gaily chattering. The pirates listened grimly, and then changed the mushroom. They appeared spherical them and referred to the holes in the seven bushes.

"did you pay attention them say peter pan's from domestic?" smee whispered, playing with johnny corkscrew. Hook nodded. He stood for a long term misplaced in notion, and at last a curdling smile lit up his swarthy face. Smee had been looking forward to it. "unrip your plan, captain," he cried eagerly.

"to head back to the ship," hook answered slowly thru his enamel, "and cook dinner dinner a massive wealthy cake of a jolly thickness with green sugar on it. There can be however one room underneath, for there may be however one chimney. The stupid moles had no longer the texture to see that they did not need a door apiece. That shows they haven't any mom. We are able to leave the cake on the shore of the mermaids' lagoon. Those boys are constantly swimming about there, playing with the mermaids. They'll locate the cake and they will gobble it up, due to the fact, having no mother, they do not know how dangerous 'tis to eat wealthy damp cake." he burst into laughter, now not hole laughter now, however honest laughter. "aha, they will die."

smee had listened with developing admiration.

"it's the wickedest, prettiest coverage ever i heard of!" he cried, and of their exultation they danced and sang:

"avast, belay, after i seem,

with the aid of way of worry they're overtook;

nought's left upon your bones whilst you

have shaken claws with hook."

they started out the verse, but they by no means finished it, for some other sound broke in and stilled them. There was within the starting this kind of tiny sound that a leaf may additionally have fallen on it and smothered it, however because it got here nearer it was greater distinct. Tick tick tick tick! Hook stood shuddering, one foot inside the air.

"the crocodile!" he gasped, and bounded away, observed via his bo'sun. It became genuinely the crocodile. It had exceeded the redskins, who have been now at the path of the alternative pirates. It oozed on after hook. Once more the men emerged into the open; but the risks of the night time were not but over, for presently nibs rushed breathless into their midst, pursued by using a p. C. Of wolves. The tongues of the pursuers have been placing out; the baying of them changed into terrible.

"save me, keep me!" cried nibs, falling at the floor.

"however what are we able to do, what are we able to do?"

it modified right into a excessive reward to peter that at that dire 2d their mind became to him.

"what should peter do?" they cried concurrently. Nearly within the equal breath they cried, "peter could study them thru his legs."

and then, "permit us to do what peter would possibly do."

it's miles pretty the maximum a success manner of defying wolves, and as one boy they bent and seemed thru their legs. The next moment is the long one, however victory got here quickly, for as the men superior upon them in the horrible attitude, the wolves dropped their tails and fled. Now nibs rose from the floor, and the others belief that his staring eyes though observed the wolves. However it became not wolves he noticed.

"i've seen a wonderfuller detail," he cried, as they gathered spherical him eagerly. "a amazing white hen. It's far flying this manner."

"what sort of a bird, do you watched?"

"i do not recognise," nibs stated, awestruck, "however it appears so weary, and as it flies it moans, 'bad wendy,'"

"terrible wendy?"

"i recall," stated barely proper away, "there are birds referred to as wendies."

"see, it comes!" cried curly, pointing to wendy inside the heavens. Wendy turned into now almost overhead, and they might concentrate her plaintive cry. However more wonderful got here the shrill voice of tinker bell. The jealous fairy had now put off all conceal of friendship, and was darting at her victim from each direction, pinching savagely on every occasion she touched.

"hullo, tink," cried the questioning boys. Tink's reply rang out: "peter wishes you to shoot the wendy."

it modified into now not of their nature to question even as peter ordered. "let us do what peter desires!" cried the easy boys. "brief, bows and arrows!"

all but tootles popped down their timber. He had a bow and arrow with him, and tink cited it, and rubbed her little palms.

"brief, tootles, short," she screamed. "peter may be so pleased."

tootles excitedly outfitted the arrow to his bow. "out of the manner, tink," he shouted, after which he fired, and wendy fluttered to the floor with an arrow in her breast.

Chapter

6

the little house

foolish tootles turned into status like a conqueror over wendy's body when the other boys sprang, armed, from their timber.

"you're too late," he cried proudly, "i have shot the wendy. Peter might be so thrilled with me."

overhead tinker bell shouted "stupid ass!" and darted into hiding. The others did not pay attention her. They'd crowded spherical wendy, and as they appeared a horrible silence fell upon the wooden. If wendy's coronary heart have been beating they might all have heard it. Barely changed into the first to talk. "this is no chook," he stated in a scared voice. "i suppose this need to be a female."

"a woman?" said tootles, and fell a-trembling.

"and we have killed her," nibs stated hoarsely. All of them whipped off their caps.

"now i see," curly stated: "peter became bringing her to us." he threw himself sorrowfully on the ground.

"a woman to take care of us at last," said one of the twins, "and you've got killed her!"

they had been sorry for him, however sorrier for themselves, and whilst he took a step nearer them they grew to become from him. Tootles' face turned into very white, but there has been a dignity about him now that had in no way been there earlier than.

"i did it," he stated, reflecting. "while girls used to return to me in goals, i said, 'pretty mom, quite mom.' however when at closing she absolutely got here, i shot her."

he moved slowly away.

"do not move," they known as in pity.

"i should," he spoke back, shaking; "i'm so fearful of peter."

it was at this tragic second that they heard a legitimate which made the heart of every one of them rise to his mouth. They heard peter crow.

"peter!" they cried, for it turned into always hence that he signalled his return.

"cover her," they whispered, and collected unexpectedly round wendy. But tootles stood aloof. Again got here that ringing crow, and peter dropped in front of them. "greetings, boys," he cried, and mechanically they saluted, and then again changed into silence. He frowned.

"i am returned," he said hotly, "why do you no longer cheer?"

they opened their mouths, but the cheers might no longer come. He not noted it in his haste to tell the wonderful tidings.

"terrific news, boys," he cried, "i've delivered at final a mother for you all."

nevertheless no sound, except a bit thud from tootles as he dropped on his knees.

"have you ever no longer seen her?" requested peter, becoming afflicted. "she flew this manner."

"ah me!" as soon as voice said, and any other stated, "oh, mournful day."

tootles rose. "peter," he stated quietly, "i will display her to you," and when the others might nevertheless have hidden her he said, "again, twins, allow peter see."

so all of them stood again, and permit him see, and after he had looked for a little time he did not realize what to do subsequent.

"she is useless," he stated uncomfortably. "possibly she is fearful at being lifeless."

he thought of hopping off in a comic sort of manner until he was out of sight of her, and then in no way going close to the spot any more. They might all have been satisfied to comply with if he had achieved this. However there was the arrow. He took it from her coronary heart and confronted his band.

"whose arrow?" he demanded sternly.

"mine, peter," stated tootles on his knees.

"oh, dastard hand," peter said, and he raised the arrow to use it as a dagger. Tootles did now not flinch. He bared his breast. "strike, peter," he stated firmly, "strike genuine."

twice did peter improve the arrow, and twice did his hand fall. "i cannot strike," he said with awe, "there is something stays my hand."

all looked at him in wonder, save nibs, who fortuitously checked out wendy.

"it's far she," he cried, "the wendy woman, see, her arm!"

exquisite to narrate [tell], wendy had raised her arm. Nibs bent over her and listened reverently. "i think she stated, 'negative tootles,'" he whispered.

"she lives," peter stated in brief. Slightly cried right away, "the wendy girl lives."

then peter knelt beside her and located his button. You take into account she had positioned it on a chain that she wore spherical her neck.

"see," he stated, "the arrow struck against this. It's far the kiss i gave her. It has stored her existence."

"i bear in mind kisses," slightly interposed quickly, "allow me see it. Ay, it really is a kiss."

peter did not listen him. He changed into begging wendy to get better quickly, so that he should display her the mermaids. Of course she could not answer yet, being still in a frightful faint; but from overhead came a wailing note.

"concentrate to tink," stated curly, "she is crying due to the fact the wendy lives."

then they'd to inform peter of tink's crime, and nearly by no means had they seen him appearance so stern.

"listen, tinker bell," he cried, "i am your pal no greater. Begone from me for ever."

she flew on to his shoulder and pleaded, but he brushed her off. Now not till wendy again raised her arm did he relent sufficiently to say, "properly, now not for ever, however for a whole week."

do you think tinker bell became grateful to wendy for elevating her arm? Oh pricey no, in no way wanted to pinch her a lot. Fairies indeed are ordinary, and peter, who understood them high-quality, regularly cuffed [slapped] them. But what to do with wendy in her present sensitive nation of fitness?

"let us carry her down into the house," curly suggested.

"ay," stated barely, "that's what one does with women."

"no, no," peter said, "you ought to not touch her. It might now not be sufficiently respectful."

"that," said slightly, "is what i was wondering."

"but if she lies there," tootles said, "she can die."

"ay, she can die," slightly admitted, "but there may be no way out."

"yes, there is," cried peter. "allow us to construct a little house round her."

they had been all overjoyed. "short," he ordered them, "deliver me every of you the best of what we've. Gut our house. Be sharp."

in a moment they were as busy as tailors the night time earlier than a marriage. They skurried this way and that, down for bedding, up for firewood, and while they had been at it, who have to appear however john and michael. As they dragged alongside the ground they fell asleep standing, stopped, awoke, moved some other step and slept again.

"john, john," michael could cry, "awaken! Wherein is nana, john, and mom?"

and then john could rub his eyes and mutter, "it is true, we did fly."

you may be certain they had been very relieved to discover peter.

"hullo, peter," they said.

"hullo," spoke back peter amicably, although he had quite forgotten them. He become very busy for the time being measuring wendy along with his toes to see how large a residence she might want. Of course he meant to go away room for chairs and a table. John and michael watched him.

"is wendy asleep?" they asked.

"sure."

"john," michael proposed, "let us wake her and get her to make supper for us," however as he stated it some of the opposite boys rushed on carrying branches for the building of the residence. "have a look at them!" he cried.

"curly," stated peter in his most captainy voice, "see that these boys assist in the building of the residence."

"ay, ay, sir."

"build a residence?" exclaimed john.

"for the wendy," said curly.

"for wendy?" john said, aghast. "why, she is best a female!"

"that," defined curly, "is why we are her servants."

"you? Wendy's servants!"

"yes," stated peter, "and also you also. Away with them."

the astounded brothers have been dragged away to hack and hew and convey. "chairs and a fender [fireplace] first," peter ordered. "then we shall build a residence round them."

"ay," stated slightly, "this is how a residence is constructed; all of it comes returned to me."

peter idea of the entirety. "barely," he cried, "fetch a medical doctor."

"ay, ay," stated barely right away, and disappeared, scratching his head. But he knew peter ought to be obeyed, and he lower back in a moment, wearing john's hat and searching solemn.

"please, sir," said peter, going to him, "are you a health practitioner?"

the distinction among him and the alternative boys at any such time changed into that they knew it become make-accept as true with, whilst to him make-accept as true with and true had been exactly the same element. This on occasion them, as once they had to make-accept as true with that they had had their dinners. If they broke down in their make-accept as true with he rapped them on the knuckles.

"yes, my little man," barely anxiously replied, who had chapped knuckles.

"please, sir," peter defined, "a woman lies very sick."

she became lying at their toes, however slightly had the sense no longer to look her.

"tut, tut, tut," he said, "wherein does she lie?"

"in yonder glade."

"i'm able to positioned a pitcher issue in her mouth," stated barely, and he made-believe to do it, even as peter waited. It was an anxious moment when the glass factor turned into withdrawn.

"how is she?" inquired peter.

"tut, tut, tut," stated barely, "this has cured her."

"i'm happy!" peter cried.

"i'm able to name once more within the night," slightly stated; "deliver her beef tea out of a cup with a spout to it;" but after he had back the hat to john he blew big breaths, which become his habit on escaping from a difficulty. In the meantime the timber had been alive with the sound of axes; nearly everything wished for a comfy dwelling already lay at wendy's ft.

"if best we knew," stated one, "the form of house she likes great."

"peter," shouted another, "she is moving in her sleep."

"her mouth opens," cried a 3rd, searching respectfully into it. "oh, lovable!"

"perhaps she is going to sing in her sleep," stated peter. "wendy, sing the kind of residence you would like to have."

immediately, without beginning her eyes, wendy started to sing:

"i wish i had a quite residence,

the littlest ever seen,

with funny little purple partitions

and roof of mossy inexperienced."

they gurgled with pleasure at this, for with the aid of the greatest desirable good fortune the branches they'd delivered have been sticky with crimson sap, and all the ground turned into carpeted with moss. As they rattled up the little house they broke into track themselves:

"we've got constructed the little walls and roof

and made a cute door,

so inform us, mom wendy,

what are you looking greater?"

to this she spoke back greedily:

"oh, sincerely subsequent i assume i will have

homosexual windows all about,

with roses peeping in, you realize,

and toddlers peeping out."

with a blow of their fists they made home windows, and large yellow leaves had been the blinds. However roses—?

"roses," cried peter sternly. Speedy they made-consider to develop the loveliest roses up the walls. Babies? To save you peter ordering infants they hurried into song again:

"we have made the roses peeping out,

the babes are at the door,

we can not make ourselves, you realize,

'cos we have been made before."

peter, seeing this to be an excellent idea, right away pretended that it became his personal. The house became quite stunning, and no doubt wendy was very snug within, even though, of course, they could no longer see her. Peter strode up and down, ordering completing touches. Nothing escaped his eagle eyes. Just whilst it regarded genuinely finished:

"there is no knocker on the door," he said. They had been very ashamed, however tootles gave the only of his shoe, and it made an superb knocker. Without a doubt finished now, they concept. No longer of bit of it. "there may be no chimney," peter said; "we have to have a chimney."

"it actually does need a chimney," stated john importantly. This gave peter an concept. He snatched the hat off john's head, knocked out the lowest [top], and put the hat on the roof. The little residence become so thrilled to have this kind of capital chimney that, as if to mention thank you, smoke straight away started to pop out of the hat. Now genuinely and honestly it turned into finished. Not anything remained to do however to knock.

"all look your first-rate," peter warned them; "first impressions are really essential."

he turned into satisfied nobody requested him what first impressions are; they were all too busy looking their pleasant. He knocked with politeness, and now the wooden changed into as still as the kids, no longer a sound to be heard besides from tinker bell, who turned into looking from a department and brazenly sneering. What the lads have been thinking became, would anyone solution the knock? If a woman, what might she be like? The door opened and a lady got here out. It became wendy. All of them whipped off their hats. She appeared nicely surprised, and this was simply how they'd hoped she might look.

"in which am i?" she said. Of route barely was the first to get his word in. "wendy girl," he said swiftly, "for you we constructed this house."

"oh, say you're thrilled," cried nibs.

"lovely, darling house," wendy said, and that they were the very phrases that they had was hoping she could say.

"and we are your children," cried the twins. Then all went on their knees, and keeping out their hands cried, "o wendy female, be our mother."

"ought i?" wendy said, all shining. "of path it is frightfully captivating, however you notice i'm most effective a little female. I have no real revel in."

"that doesn't remember," stated peter, as if he were the handiest individual present who knew all about it, although he turned into definitely the one who knew least. "what we need is simply a pleasant motherly man or woman."

"oh expensive!" wendy stated, "you notice, i sense this is exactly what i am."

"it is, it is," all of them cried; "we noticed it right now."

"thoroughly," she said, "i can do my high-quality. Come inner right away, you naughty kids; i'm sure your ft are damp. And earlier than i placed you to bed i have simply time to complete the tale of cinderella."

in they went; i do not know how there has been room for them, however you can squeeze very tight inside the neverland. And that turned into the primary of the many joyous evenings that they had with wendy. With the aid of and by she tucked them up in the incredible mattress within the domestic underneath the trees, however she herself slept that night within the little house, and peter stored watch outside with drawn sword, for the pirates might be heard carousing a long way away and the wolves have been on the prowl. The little residence regarded so snug and safe in the darkness, with a bright mild showing thru its blinds, and the chimney smoking superbly, and peter standing on guard. After a time he fell asleep, and a few unsteady fairies needed to climb over him on their way domestic from an orgy. Any of the other boys obstructing the fairy route at night they might have mischiefed, however they simply tweaked peter's nose and surpassed on.

Chapter

7

one of the first matters peter did subsequent day turned into to degree wendy and john and michael for hollow timber. Hook, you don't forget, had sneered at the boys for wondering they wished a tree apiece, but this was lack of knowledge, for unless your tree equipped you it changed into tough to move up and down, and no of the lads were pretty the equal size. After you geared up, you drew in [let out] your breath at the pinnacle, and down you went at exactly the proper velocity, at the same time as to ascend you drew in and let loose alternately, and so wriggled up. Of course, when you have mastered the movement you're able to do this stuff with out taking into consideration them, and nothing can be greater swish. But you in reality should healthy, and peter measures you to your tree as carefully as for a match of clothes: the simplest difference being that the garments are made to suit you, while you have to be made to match the tree. Normally it's miles performed quite without difficulty, as by using your wearing too many clothes or too few, however in case you are bumpy in awkward places or the simplest available tree is an odd form, peter does a few things to you, and after which you healthy. Once you suit, amazing care must be taken to head on becoming, and this, as wendy turned into to discover to her pride, maintains an entire family in best circumstance. Wendy and michael equipped their trees at the primary attempt, however john needed to be altered a bit. After some days' exercise they might go up and down as gaily as buckets in a well. And how ardently they grew to love their home under the ground; particularly wendy. It consisted of 1 huge room, as all houses have to do, with a floor wherein you can dig [for worms] if you wanted to move fishing, and on this ground grew stout mushrooms of a captivating coloration, which had been used as stools. A by no means tree attempted difficult to grow within the centre of the room, however each morning they sawed the trunk thru, level with the ground. Via tea-time it became usually approximately ft high, and then they positioned a door on pinnacle of it, the whole hence becoming a desk; as soon as they cleared away, they sawed off the trunk again, and therefore there has been greater room to play. There has been an widespread fireplace which changed into in almost any part of the room in which you cared to light it, and throughout this wendy stretched strings, product of fibre, from which she suspended her washing. The mattress turned into tilted in opposition to the wall via day, and let down at 6:30, while it stuffed almost half the room; and all the boys slept in it, besides michael, mendacity like sardines in a tin. There was a strict rule towards turning round until one gave the signal, while all turned straight away. Michael have to have used it also, but wendy could have [desired] a toddler, and he become the littlest, and what women are, and the quick and long of it's far that he became hung up in a basket. It changed into rough and easy, and now not in contrast to what toddler bears might have made of an underground house within the identical situations. However there has been one recess within the wall, no larger than a chook-cage, which become the non-public rental of tinker bell. It can be close off from the relaxation of the house via a tiny curtain, which tink, who changed into maximum fastidious [particular], always stored drawn while dressing or undressing. No girl, but massive, may want to have had a extra high-quality boudoir [dressing room] and mattress-chamber mixed. The sofa, as she constantly known as it, become a genuine queen mab, with membership legs; and she or he varied the bedspreads in line with what fruit-blossom changed into in season. Her replicate turned into a puss-in-boots, of which there are actually most effective three, unchipped, known to fairy dealers; the washstand changed into pie-crust and reversible, the chest of drawers an real captivating the 6th, and the carpet and rugs the great (the early) period of margery and robin. There was a chandelier from tiddlywinks for the look of the component, however of path she lit the house herself. Tink changed into very contemptuous of the rest of the residence, as certainly changed into perhaps inevitable, and her chamber, even though beautiful, looked as an alternative immodest, having the appearance of a nose completely grew to become up. I assume it became all specifically entrancing to wendy, due to the fact the ones rampagious boys of hers gave her a lot to do. Without a doubt there had been whole weeks whilst, besides possibly with a stocking in the nighttime, she was in no way above ground. The cooking, i will inform you, saved her nostril to the pot, and even if there has been nothing in it, even if there was no pot, she needed to keep watching that it got here aboil simply the same. You never precisely knew whether there could be a actual meal or only a make-accept as true with, all of it depended upon peter's whim: he ought to devour, genuinely consume, if it was a part of a sport, however he couldn't stodge [cram down the food] just to experience stodgy [stuffed with food], which is what most youngsters like higher than anything else; the subsequent exceptional element being to speak about it. Make-accept as true with turned into so actual to him that during a meal of it you can see him getting rounder. Of course it become attempting, however you definitely needed to follow his lead, and if you may show to him which you had been getting free on your tree he will let you stodge. Wendy's favored time for sewing and darning became once they had all long gone to bed. Then, as she expressed it, she had a breathing time for herself; and she or he occupied it in making new things for them, and setting double pieces on the knees, for they were all maximum frightfully difficult on their knees. Whilst she sat right down to a basketful of their stockings, every heel with a hollow in it, she could fling up her hands and exclaim, "oh dear, i am positive i every so often think spinsters are to be envied!"

her face beamed whilst she exclaimed this. You do not forget approximately her pet wolf. Properly, it very soon located that she had come to the island and it found her out, and that they simply ran into each other's arms. After that it accompanied her approximately anywhere. As time wore on did she assume tons about the loved mother and father she had left behind her? This is a hard query, due to the fact it's far pretty not possible to say how time does wear on inside the neverland, in which it's far calculated by way of moons and suns, and there are ever so many extra of them than on the mainland. However i am afraid that wendy did now not genuinely worry approximately her parents; she became simply confident that they might constantly maintain the window open for her to fly back by, and this gave her entire ease of thoughts. What did disturb her at times was that john remembered his parents vaguely best, as humans he had as soon as known, whilst michael became pretty inclined to agree with that she become surely his mother. These items scared her a little, and nobly annoying to do her responsibility, she attempted to repair the antique life in their minds by putting them examination papers on it, as like as viable to those she used to do at school. The alternative boys concept this tremendously thrilling, and insisted on joining, and that they made slates for themselves, and sat round the table, writing and thinking difficult approximately the questions she had written on some other slate and handed spherical. They had been the most ordinary questions—"what became the shade of mom's eyes? Which become taller, mother or father? Turned into mother blonde or brunette? Answer all three questions if feasible." "(a) write an essay of now not much less than 40 phrases on how i spent my closing vacations, or the characters of moms and dads as compared. Simplest such a to be tried." or "(1) describe mother's snigger; (2) describe father's chuckle; (three) describe mom's party dress; (4) describe the kennel and its inmate."

they were simply normal questions like these, and whilst you could not solution them you have been advised to make a go; and it become truely dreadful what some of crosses even john made. Of path the only boy who replied to each query become slightly, and nobody could have been extra hopeful of coming out first, however his answers had been flawlessly ridiculous, and he actually came out last: a depression component. Peter did not compete. For one aspect he despised all moms except wendy, and for any other he turned into the simplest boy at the island who may want to neither write nor spell; now not the smallest phrase. He become certainly that kind of element. By the manner, the questions were all written inside the beyond irritating. What turned into the shade of mother's eyes, and so forth. Wendy, you notice, had been forgetting, too. Adventures, of direction, as we shall see, had been of daily occurrence; however approximately this time peter invented, with wendy's help, a brand new recreation that involved him quite, till he had no greater interest in it, which, as you have got been instructed, became what usually occurred with his video games. It consisted in pretending no longer to have adventures, in doing the kind of aspect john and michael have been doing all their lives, sitting on stools flinging balls in the air, pushing each other, going out for walks and coming back while not having killed a lot as a grizzly. To look peter doing nothing on a stool was a extremely good sight; he could not assist looking solemn at such instances, to take a seat still regarded to him one of these comic issue to do. He boasted that he had long past taking walks for the good of his health. For several suns these were the maximum novel of all adventures to him; and john and michael needed to fake to be thrilled additionally; otherwise he might have handled them severely. He frequently went out by myself, and while he got here back you had been in no way genuinely certain whether or not he had had an journey or no longer. He may have forgotten it so absolutely that he said nothing about it; after which whilst you went out you found the body; and, however, he may say a fantastic deal approximately it, and yet you could not locate the body. Every so often he got here domestic along with his head bandaged, after which wendy cooed over him and bathed it in lukewarm water, whilst he told a astonishing story. But she became never pretty certain, . There have been, but, many adventures which she knew to be true due to the fact she turned into in them herself, and there were nonetheless extra that were at least in part proper, for the opposite boys had been in them and stated they have been thoroughly true. To explain all of them could require a book as big as an english-latin, latin-english dictionary, and the most we can do is to offer one as a specimen of a mean hour on the island. The problem is which one to pick. Must we take the comb with the redskins at slightly gulch? It turned into a sanguinary [cheerful] affair, and in particular interesting as showing one of peter's peculiarities, which was that within the middle of a fight he could unexpectedly change aspects. At the gulch, when victory turned into nevertheless inside the balance, every now and then leaning this manner and sometimes that, he called out, "i'm redskin to-day; what are you, tootles?" and tootles answered, "redskin; what are you, nibs?" and nibs stated, "redskin; what are you dual?" and so on; and they had been all redskins; and of route this will have ended the fight had no longer the actual redskins inquisitive about peter's methods, agreed to be misplaced boys for that once, and so at it they all went again, more fiercely than ever. The extraordinary upshot of this adventure changed into—but we've got now not determined yet that that is the adventure we're to narrate. Perhaps a higher one will be the night assault by the redskins on the house below the ground, while several of them stuck within the hollow bushes and had to be pulled out like corks. Or we might tell how peter stored tiger lily's existence within the mermaids' lagoon, and so made her his ally. Or we could inform of that cake the pirates cooked in order that the boys would possibly consume it and perish; and the way they located it in one cunning spot after any other; but always wendy snatched it from the fingers of her youngsters, so that in time it misplaced its succulence, and have become as difficult as a stone, and turned into used as a missile, and hook fell over it within the dark. Or assume we inform of the birds that have been peter's pals, in particular of the in no way fowl that constructed in a tree overhanging the lagoon, and how the nest fell into the water, and nonetheless the hen sat on her eggs, and peter gave orders that she changed into not to be disturbed. That is a pretty story, and the cease shows how thankful a bird may be; but if we tell it we should additionally inform the complete journey of the lagoon, which would of direction be telling adventures in preference to simply one. A shorter adventure, and quite as interesting, became tinker bell's attempt, with the help of a few road fairies, to have the sound asleep wendy conveyed on a first-rate floating leaf to the mainland. Thankfully the leaf gave manner and wendy woke, thinking it was tub-time, and swam again. Or once more, we would select peter's defiance of the lions, when he drew a circle spherical him at the ground with an arrow and dared them to pass it; and even though he waited for hours, with the other boys and wendy searching on breathlessly from bushes, now not considered one of them dared to accept his mission. Which of those adventures shall we pick? The quality way might be to toss for it. I have tossed, and the lagoon has won. This nearly makes one wish that the gulch or the cake or tink's leaf had won. Of direction i may want to do it again, and make it exceptional out of 3; but, possibly fairest to paste to the lagoon.

Chapter

8

if you close your eyes and are a lucky one, you could see at instances a shapeless pool of adorable pale shades suspended inside the darkness; then if you squeeze your eyes tighter, the pool starts offevolved to take form, and the colors end up so bright that with any other squeeze they ought to move on fire. But just earlier than they go on hearth you see the lagoon. This is the nearest you ever get to it at the mainland, simply one heavenly second; if there may be moments you would possibly see the surf and listen the mermaids singing. The kids frequently spent long summer season days on this lagoon, swimming or floating maximum of the time, playing the mermaid video games inside the water, and so on. You must no longer think from this that the mermaids were on friendly terms with them: on the opposite, it turned into amongst wendy's lasting regrets that every one the time she turned into at the island she in no way had a civil phrase from one in every of them. Whilst she stole softly to the threshold of the lagoon she may see them by way of the rating, particularly on marooners' rock, wherein they cherished to bask, combing out their hair in a lazy manner that pretty indignant her; or she would possibly even swim, on tiptoe because it have been, to within a yard of them, but then they saw her and dived, probable splashing her with their tails, now not with the aid of twist of fate, but deliberately. They treated all of the boys inside the equal way, besides of course peter, who chatted with them on marooners' rock by way of the hour, and sat on their tails once they got cheeky. He gave wendy one among their combs. The most haunting time at which to look them is on the flip of the moon, after they utter abnormal wailing cries; but the lagoon is dangerous for mortals then, and until the evening of which we have now to inform, wendy had never visible the lagoon with the aid of moonlight, less from fear, for of path peter would have observed her, than because she had strict regulations about each one being in mattress through seven. She was regularly at the lagoon, but, on sunny days after rain, whilst the mermaids arise in incredible numbers to play with their bubbles. The bubbles of many colors made in rainbow water they treat as balls, hitting them gaily from one to another with their tails, and trying to hold them inside the rainbow until they burst. The goals are at every quit of the rainbow, and the keepers only are allowed to use their arms. Every now and then a dozen of those video games will be taking place in the lagoon at a time, and it's miles quite a pretty sight. However the second the children tried to join in they had to play by means of themselves, for the mermaids immediately disappeared. Nevertheless we've proof that they secretly watched the interlopers, and were not above taking an concept from them; for john introduced a new manner of hitting the bubble, with the head as opposed to the hand, and the mermaids adopted it. This is the one mark that john has left at the neverland. It ought to additionally were as an alternative quite to peer the children resting on a rock for half of an hour after their mid-day meal. Wendy insisted on their doing this, and it had to be a actual relaxation despite the fact that the meal was make-accept as true with. In order that they lay there within the sun, and their bodies glistened in it, at the same time as she sat beside them and regarded important. It changed into one such day, and they had been all on marooners' rock. The rock was now not lots larger than their brilliant bed, however of path they all knew how not to take in an awful lot room, and they have been sound asleep, or as a minimum mendacity with their eyes shut, and pinching on occasion after they concept wendy was now not looking. She changed into very busy, sewing. Even as she stitched a trade got here to the lagoon. Little shivers ran over it, and the sun went away and shadows stole throughout the water, turning it bloodless. Wendy ought to not see to string her needle, and whilst she looked up, the lagoon that had continually hitherto been this kind of giggling vicinity regarded bold and unfriendly. It become now not, she knew, that night had come, but something as darkish as night time had come. No, worse than that. It had no longer come, however it had despatched that shiver thru the sea to mention that it was coming. What changed into it? There crowded upon her all the tales she have been informed of marooners' rock, so referred to as due to the fact evil captains positioned sailors on it and go away them there to drown. They drown when the tide rises, for then it's miles submerged. Of course she need to have roused the youngsters straight away; not simply due to the unknown that turned into stalking closer to them, but because it turned into not properly for them to sleep on a rock grown chilly. But she become a younger mother and she or he did now not understand this; she concept you honestly must stick with your rule approximately half an hour after the mid-day meal. So, although worry was upon her, and she longed to listen male voices, she could now not waken them. Even when she heard the sound of muffled oars, though her coronary heart become in her mouth, she did no longer waken them. She stood over them to allow them to have their sleep out. Changed into it now not courageous of wendy? It was properly for those boys then that there has been one among them who may want to sniff hazard even in his sleep. Peter sprang erect, as extensive awake at once as a dog, and with one caution cry he roused the others. He stood motionless, one hand to his ear.

"pirates!" he cried. The others came in the direction of him. A atypical smile became playing about his face, and wendy saw it and shuddered. While that smile was on his face no one dared address him; all they could do turned into to stand geared up to obey. The order came sharp and incisive.

"dive!"

there was a gleam of legs, and immediately the lagoon regarded deserted. Marooners' rock stood by myself within the forbidding waters as though it had been itself marooned. The boat drew nearer. It turned into the pirate dinghy, with 3 figures in her, smee and starkey, and the 1/3 a captive, no aside from tiger lily. Her fingers and ankles had been tied, and she or he knew what became to be her fate. She become to be left at the rock to perish, an end to considered one of her race greater terrible than death via fire or torture, for is it now not written inside the e-book of the tribe that there is no course thru water to the glad looking-floor? But her face become emotionless; she became the daughter of a main, she need to die as a primary's daughter, it's miles sufficient. That they had caught her boarding the pirate ship with a knife in her mouth. No watch was kept on the ship, it being hook's boast that the wind of his call guarded the deliver for a mile round. Now her fate would help to guard it additionally. One extra wail would pass the round in that wind through night. Within the gloom that they introduced with them the two pirates did now not see the rock until they crashed into it.

"luff, you lubber," cried an irish voice that turned into smee's; "right here's the rock. Now, then, what we should do is to hoist the redskin on to it and go away her right here to drown."

it changed into the work of 1 brutal moment to land the beautiful girl on the rock; she become too proud to offer a vain resistance. Quite close to the rock, however out of sight, two heads had been bobbing up and down, peter's and wendy's. Wendy turned into crying, for it was the primary tragedy she had seen. Peter had seen many tragedies, however he had forgotten them all. He become less sorry than wendy for tiger lily: it was in opposition to one which angered him, and he meant to shop her. An easy manner could were to attend till the pirates had long gone, but he was never one to choose the easy manner. There was nearly nothing he could not do, and he now imitated the voice of hook.

"ahoy there, you lubbers!" he referred to as. It became a marvellous imitation.

"the captain!" said the pirates, gazing every other in wonder.

"he ought to be swimming out to us," starkey stated, once they had looked for him in useless.

"we are setting the redskin at the rock," smee called out.

"set her loose," got here the awesome answer.

"loose!"

"yes, cut her bonds and let her move."

"but, captain—"

"right now, d'ye pay attention," cried peter, "or i will plunge my hook in you."

"that is queer!" smee gasped.

"better do what the captain orders," stated starkey nervously.

"ay, ay." smee stated, and he reduce tiger lily's cords. Straight away like an eel she slid between starkey's legs into the water. Of course wendy was very elated over peter's cleverness; however she knew that he might be elated additionally and really in all likelihood crow and accordingly betray himself, so at once her hand went out to cowl his mouth. However it turned into stayed even inside the act, for "boat ahoy!" rang over the lagoon in hook's voice, and this time it become not peter who had spoken. Peter may also had been about to crow, but his face puckered in a whistle of marvel rather.

"boat ahoy!" again came the voice. Now wendy understood. The real hook turned into also in the water. He became swimming to the boat, and as his guys showed a light to manual him he had soon reached them. In the light of the lantern wendy noticed his hook grip the boat's side; she saw his evil swarthy face as he rose dripping from the water, and, quaking, she would have preferred to swim away, but peter might no longer budge. He changed into tingling with lifestyles and additionally top-heavy with conceit. "am i now not a marvel, oh, i'm a surprise!" he whispered to her, and even though she concept so additionally, she became really satisfied for the sake of his popularity that no person heard him besides herself. He signed to her to concentrate. The two pirates were very curious to recognise what had introduced their captain to them, but he sat together with his head on his hook in a function of profound despair.

"captain, is all well?" they requested timidly, however he spoke back with a hole moan.

"he sighs," said smee.

"he sighs again," stated starkey.

"and but a 3rd time he sighs," said smee. Then at ultimate he spoke passionately.

"the sport's up," he cried, "those boys have discovered a mom."

affrighted although she became, wendy swelled with satisfaction.

"o evil day!" cried starkey.

"what is a mom?" asked the ignorant smee. Wendy become so taken aback that she exclaimed. "he does not know!" and always after this she felt that if you could have a pet pirate smee would be her one. Peter pulled her underneath the water, for hook had began up, crying, "what was that?"

"i heard nothing," said starkey, elevating the lantern over the waters, and because the pirates looked they noticed a odd sight. It became the nest i have advised you of, floating at the lagoon, and the by no means chook become sitting on it.

"see," stated hook in solution to smee's question, "that is a mom. What a lesson! The nest need to have fallen into the water, but could the mother desolate tract her eggs? No."

there was a ruin in his voice, as if for a moment he recalled innocent days while—but he brushed away this weakness together with his hook. Smee, a good deal inspired, gazed on the chicken as the nest become borne beyond, but the more suspicious starkey stated, "if she is a mother, perhaps she is striking about here to help peter."

hook winced. "ay," he stated, "this is the fear that haunts me."

he became roused from this dejection by smee's eager voice.

"captain," stated smee, "may want to we now not kidnap these boys' mother and make her our mom?"

"it is a princely scheme," cried hook, and right now it took sensible form in his first rate brain. "we can capture the kids and deliver them to the boat: the boys we will make stroll the plank, and wendy will be our mother."

once more wendy forgot herself.

"in no way!" she cried, and bobbed.

"what become that?"

but they may see nothing. They thought it ought to were a leaf inside the wind. "do you agree, my bullies?" asked hook.

"there's my hand on it," they each said.

"and there's my hook. Swear."

all of them swore. Via this time they had been on the rock, and all of sudden hook remembered tiger lily.

"in which is the redskin?" he demanded unexpectedly. He had a playful humour at moments, and that they concept this became one of the moments.

"this is all right, captain," smee answered complacently; "we let her move."

"permit her pass!" cried hook.

"'twas your own orders," the bo'sun faltered.

"you called over the water to us to let her move," said starkey.

"brimstone and gall," thundered hook, "what cozening [cheating] is going on right here!" his face had long gone black with rage, but he noticed that they believed their words, and he become startled. "lads," he stated, shaking a little, "i gave no such order."

"it is passing queer," smee said, and all of them fidgeted uncomfortably. Hook raised his voice, but there was a quiver in it.

"spirit that haunts this darkish lagoon to-night," he cried, "dost pay attention me?"

of path peter ought to have kept quiet, however of route he did no longer. He without delay answered in hook's voice:

"odds, bobs, hammer and tongs, i hear you."

in that best second hook did now not blanch, even at the gills, but smee and starkey clung to each different in terror.

"who're you, stranger? Speak!" hook demanded.

"i am james hook," spoke back the voice, "captain of the jolly roger."

"you are not; you aren't," hook cried hoarsely.

"brimstone and gall," the voice retorted, "say that once more, and i will forged anchor in you."

hook tried a extra ingratiating way. "if you are hook," he said almost humbly, "come tell me, who am i?"

"a codfish," replied the voice, "only a codfish."

"a codfish!" hook echoed blankly, and it turned into then, but now not until then, that his proud spirit broke. He saw his guys pull away from him.

"have we been captained all this time with the aid of a codfish!" they muttered. "it's miles decreasing to our delight."

they were his puppies snapping at him, but, tragic determine although he had turn out to be, he scarcely heeded them. Against such nervous proof it become now not their belief in him that he needed, it changed into his personal. He felt his ego slipping from him. "do not barren region me, bully," he whispered hoarsely to it. In his darkish nature there was a hint of the feminine, as in all the super pirates, and it sometimes gave him intuitions. All of sudden he attempted the guessing recreation.

"hook," he known as, "have you ever every other voice?"

now peter could in no way face up to a sport, and he answered blithely in his personal voice, "i have."

"and any other call?"

"ay, ay."

"vegetable?" requested hook.

"no."

"mineral?"

"no."

"animal?"

"yes."

"man?"

"no!" this solution rang out scornfully.

"boy?"

"yes."

"regular boy?"

"no!"

"fantastic boy?"

to wendy's ache the solution that rang out this time turned into "sure."

"are you in england?"

"no."

"are you right here?"

"yes."

hook was completely confused. "you ask him a few questions," he said to the others, wiping his damp brow. Smee contemplated. "i cannot think about a aspect," he said regretfully.

"can not guess, can't bet!" crowed peter. "do you provide it up?"

of path in his delight he was wearing the game too some distance, and the miscreants [villains] noticed their risk.

"yes, sure," they answered eagerly.

"nicely, then," he cried, "i'm peter pan."

pan! In a second hook turned into himself once more, and smee and starkey have been his trustworthy henchmen.

"now we've got him," hook shouted. "into the water, smee. Starkey, mind the boat. Take him lifeless or alive!"

he leaped as he spoke, and simultaneously came the gay voice of peter.

"are you ready, boys?"

"ay, ay," from various components of the lagoon.

"then lam into the pirates."

the fight turned into brief and sharp. First to attract blood was john, who gallantly climbed into the boat and held starkey. There has been fierce struggle, in which the cutlass became torn from the pirate's draw close. He wriggled overboard and john leapt after him. The dinghy drifted away. Here and there a head bobbed up within the water, and there was a flash of steel accompanied through a cry or a whoop. Within the confusion some struck at their personal facet. The corkscrew of smee were given tootles in the fourth rib, but he became himself pinked [nicked] in turn by using curly. Further from the rock starkey was urgent slightly and the twins hard. Where all this time become peter? He became in search of larger game. The others had been all courageous boys, and they have to not be blamed for backing from the pirate captain. His iron claw made a circle of dead water spherical him, from which they fled like affrighted fishes. However there was person who did no longer fear him: there was one prepared to go into that circle. Surprisingly, it became no longer in the water that they met. Hook rose to the rock to respire, and on the equal moment peter scaled it on the opposite aspect. The rock became slippery as a ball, and they had to move slowly instead of climb. Neither knew that the alternative become coming. Each feeling for a grip met the other's arm: in surprise they raised their heads; their faces have been nearly touching; so that they met. A number of the greatest heroes have confessed that simply earlier than they fell to [began combat] they'd a sinking [feeling in the stomach]. Had it been so with peter at that moment i would admit it. In any case, he turned into the most effective man that the ocean-cook dinner had feared. But peter had no sinking, he had one feeling simplest, gladness; and he gnashed his pretty teeth with joy. Short as idea he snatched a knife from hook's belt and turned into approximately to force it home, when he noticed that he changed into better up the rock that his foe. It'd no longer have been fighting fair. He gave the pirate a hand to assist him up. It was then that hook bit him. Now not the ache of this however its unfairness was what dazed peter. It made him quite helpless. He could most effective stare, horrified. Each child is affected for this reason the first time he's dealt with unfairly. All he thinks he has a right to while he involves you to be yours is fairness. After you've got been unfair to him he's going to love you once more, however will in no way afterwards be pretty the equal boy. No person ever gets over the first unfairness; nobody besides peter. He frequently met it, but he constantly forgot it. I think that changed into the actual distinction between him and all the relaxation. So while he met it now it become just like the first time; and he should just stare, helpless. Two times the iron hand clawed him. A few moments afterwards the alternative boys noticed hook within the water putting wildly for the deliver; no elation on the pestilent face now, best white worry, for the crocodile changed into in dogged pursuit of him. On normal events the lads might have swum alongside cheering; however now they were uneasy, for they had misplaced both peter and wendy, and have been scouring the lagoon for them, calling them by means of call. They discovered the dinghy and went home in it, shouting "peter, wendy" as they went, however no answer came save mocking laughter from the mermaids. "they should be swimming lower back or flying," the men concluded. They had been now not very traumatic, due to the fact they had such faith in peter. They chuckled, boylike, because they might be past due for bed; and it changed into all mom wendy's fault! When their voices died away there came cold silence over the lagoon, after which a feeble cry.

"assist, help!"

two small figures had been beating towards the rock; the woman had fainted and lay at the boy's arm. With a last attempt peter pulled her up the rock after which lay down beside her. At the same time as he additionally fainted he saw that the water become rising. He knew that they could quickly be drowned, but he could do no more. As they lay side by side a mermaid caught wendy with the aid of the feet, and started pulling her softly into the water. Peter, feeling her slip from him, woke with a start, and turned into just in time to attract her again. However he had to inform her the fact.

"we are on the rock, wendy," he stated, "but it is developing smaller. Soon the water will be over it."

she did no longer apprehend even now.

"we ought to pass," she stated, nearly brightly.

"yes," he replied faintly.

"we could swim or fly, peter?"

he had to tell her.

"do you watched you can swim or fly as some distance because the island, wendy, without my assist?"

she had to admit that she become too tired. He moaned.

"what's it?" she asked, traumatic about him at once.

"i cannot assist you, wendy. Hook wounded me. I can neither fly nor swim."

"do you imply we shall both be drowned?"

"appearance how the water is rising."

they placed their palms over their eyes to shut out the sight. They concept they might soon be no more. As they sat for this reason some thing brushed against peter as mild as a kiss, and stayed there, as though announcing timidly, "can i be of any use?"

it changed into the tail of a kite, which michael had made some days before. It had torn itself out of his hand and floated away.

"michael's kite," peter said without interest, however next moment he had seized the tail, and turned into pulling the kite toward him.

"it lifted michael off the floor," he cried; "why should it not deliver you?"

"each of us!"

"it can not carry two; michael and curly tried."

"allow us to draw lots," wendy said bravely.

"and you a lady; in no way." already he had tied the tail spherical her. She clung to him; she refused to head without him; however with a "good-bye, wendy," he driven her from the rock; and in a few minutes she become borne out of his sight. Peter was on my own on the lagoon. The rock become very small now; quickly it'd be submerged. Light rays of light tiptoed throughout the waters; and through and by there has been to be heard a legitimate without delay the maximum musical and the most despair within the international: the mermaids calling to the moon. Peter changed into not quite like different boys; however he turned into afraid at ultimate. A tremour ran through him, like a shudder passing over the ocean; but on the ocean one shudder follows some other till there are loads of them, and peter felt just the only. Next second he became status erect on the rock once more, with that smile on his face and a drum beating inside him. It was announcing, "to die might be a very big adventure."

Chapter

9

the remaining sound peter heard before he turned into pretty alone had been the mermaids retiring one by one to their bedchambers underneath the ocean. He changed into too far away to listen their doorways shut; but every door inside the coral caves where they stay earrings a tiny bell whilst it opens or closes (as in all of the nicest houses at the mainland), and he heard the bells. Regularly the waters rose till they have been nibbling at his toes; and to pass the time till they made their very last gulp, he watched the handiest component at the lagoon. He thought it changed into a chunk of floating paper, perhaps part of the kite, and puzzled idly how long it would take to glide ashore. Currently he observed as an atypical factor that it changed into absolutely out upon the lagoon with some particular purpose, for it become preventing the tide, and once in a while winning; and while it won, peter, usually sympathetic to the weaker facet, couldn't assist clapping; it changed into the sort of gallant piece of paper. It turned into now not absolutely a piece of paper; it become the by no means chook, making determined efforts to reach peter on the nest. Through operating her wings, in a way she had discovered since the nest fell into the water, she became capable of some extent to guide her odd craft, but by the time peter recognized her she became very exhausted. She had come to keep him, to provide him her nest, though there had been eggs in it. I rather surprise at the chicken, for although he have been exceptional to her, he had also every now and then tormented her. I'm able to think best that, like mrs. Darling and the relaxation of them, she became melted because he had all his first enamel. She called out to him what she had come for, and he referred to as out to her what she turned into doing there; but of course neither of them understood the opposite's language. In fanciful stories human beings can communicate to the birds freely, and that i desire for the instant i ought to fake that this had been the sort of tale, and say that peter responded intelligently to the in no way bird; but reality is pleasant, and that i need to inform you most effective what certainly took place. Properly, no longer most effective may want to they now not recognize each different, but they forgot their manners.

"i—want—you—to—get—into—the—nest," the fowl called, speaking as slowly and surprisingly as feasible, "and—then—you—can—waft—ashore, but—i—am—too—worn-out—to—bring—it—any—nearer—so—you—ought to—try to—swim—to—it."

"what are you quacking about?" peter replied. "why don't you allow the nest go with the flow as typical?"

"i—want—you—" the fowl stated, and repeated it all over. Then peter tried slow and distinct.

"what—are—you—quacking—approximately?" and so forth. The in no way hen have become irritated; they have very short tempers.

"you dunderheaded little jay," she screamed, "why don't you do as i inform you?"

peter felt that she was calling him names, and at a task he retorted hotly:

"so are you!"

then as a substitute apparently they both snapped out the same statement:

"shut up!"

"shut up!"

nonetheless the bird changed into decided to shop him if she ought to, and by means of one remaining effective attempt she propelled the nest towards the rock. Then up she flew; deserting her eggs, in an effort to make her which means clear. Then at final he understood, and clutched the nest and waved his thanks to the chicken as she fluttered overhead. It became no longer to acquire his thanks, however, that she hung there in the sky; it become no longer even to observe him get into the nest; it turned into to look what he did along with her eggs. There were big white eggs, and peter lifted them up and meditated. The fowl protected her face along with her wings, in order not to peer the closing of them; but she couldn't help peeping between the feathers. I forget about whether or not i've informed you that there was a stave at the rock, driven into it by using a few buccaneers of long in the past to mark the site of buried treasure. The children had found the glittering hoard, and when in a mischievous mood used to fling showers of moidores, diamonds, pearls and pieces of 8 to the gulls, who pounced upon them for meals, and then flew away, raging at the scurvy trick that had been played upon them. The stave become nevertheless there, and on it starkey had hung his hat, a deep tarpaulin, watertight, with a large brim. Peter positioned the eggs into this hat and set it at the lagoon. It floated fantastically. The by no means bird noticed immediately what he turned into up to, and screamed her admiration of him; and, alas, peter crowed his settlement together with her. Then he were given into the nest, reared the stave in it as a mast, and hung up his shirt for a sail. On the identical moment the chook fluttered down upon the hat and all over again sat snugly on her eggs. She drifted in a single course, and he become borne off in some other, both cheering. Of direction whilst peter landed he beached his barque [small ship, actually the never bird's nest in this particular case in point] in a place where the chook might effortlessly discover it; however the hat became this kind of wonderful fulfillment that she abandoned the nest. It drifted approximately until it went to portions, and often starkey came to the shore of the lagoon, and with many bitter feelings watched the hen sitting on his hat. As we will no longer see her once more, it can be worth mentioning right here that every one never birds now build in that shape of nest, with a extensive brim on which the youngsters take an airing. Incredible were the rejoicings when peter reached the home beneath the floor almost as quickly as wendy, who had been carried hither and thither by the kite. Every boy had adventures to tell; however possibly the largest adventure of all was that they were numerous hours past due for mattress. This so inflated them that they did diverse dodgy matters to get staying up nevertheless longer, inclusive of demanding bandages; but wendy, though glorying in having all of them home once more safe and sound, changed into scandalised with the aid of the lateness of the hour, and cried, "to bed, to mattress," in a voice that had to be obeyed. Next day, but, she changed into highly soft, and gave out bandages to each one, and that they performed till mattress-time at limping approximately and sporting their hands in slings.

Chapter

10

the happy domestic

one crucial end result of the brush [with the pirates] at the lagoon become that it made the redskins their pals. Peter had saved tiger lily from a dreadful destiny, and now there has been nothing she and her braves might now not do for him. All night time they sat above, maintaining watch over the home below the floor and anticipating the massive attack with the aid of the pirates which glaringly couldn't be much longer not on time. Even by way of day they hung about, smoking the pipe of peace, and looking nearly as though they wanted tit-bits to eat. They known as peter the incredible white father, prostrating themselves [lying down] before him; and he appreciated this distinctly, in order that it changed into now not really true for him.

"the incredible white father," he could say to them in a completely lordly way, as they grovelled at his feet, "is glad to look the piccaninny warriors protective his wigwam from the pirates."

"me tiger lily," that lovely creature could reply. "peter pan shop me, me his velly excellent friend. Me no allow pirates harm him."

she changed into far too pretty to flinch on this way, but peter notion it his due, and he could answer condescendingly, "it is ideal. Peter pan has spoken."

always when he stated, "peter pan has spoken," it supposed that they have to now shut up, and that they commonplace it humbly in that spirit; but they had been in no way so respectful to the opposite boys, whom they regarded upon as simply normal braves. They stated "how-do?" to them, and such things as that; and what annoyed the boys become that peter seemed to suppose this all proper. Secretly wendy sympathised with them a bit, however she become a long way too loyal a housewife to concentrate to any court cases towards father. "father is aware of excellent," she usually said, some thing her personal opinion should be. Her personal opinion turned into that the redskins should not name her a squaw. We've now reached the night that became to be recognized among them because the night of nights, due to its adventures and their upshot. The day, as though quietly gathering its forces, had been almost uneventful, and now the redskins in their blankets have been at their posts above, while, beneath, the kids had been having their night meal; all except peter, who had long past out to get the time. The manner you bought the time at the island become to locate the crocodile, after which live close to him till the clock struck. The meal happened to be a make-accept as true with tea, and that they sat across the board, guzzling of their greed; and definitely, what with their chatter and recriminations, the noise, as wendy said, became positively deafening. To make sure, she did now not thoughts noise, but she without a doubt would no longer have them grabbing matters, after which excusing themselves by means of saying that tootles had driven their elbow. There has been a fixed rule that they should in no way hit lower back at food, but ought to refer the matter of dispute to wendy by way of raising the proper arm courteously and saying, "i complain of so-and-so;" however what commonly took place changed into that they forgot to try this or did it too much.

"silence," cried wendy whilst for the 20 th time she had instructed them that they had been no longer all to talk straight away. "is your mug empty, slightly darling?"

"now not quite empty, mummy," barely stated, after searching into an imaginary mug.

"he hasn't even started to drink his milk," nibs interposed. This became telling, and slightly seized his danger.

"i complain of nibs," he cried right away. John, however, had held up his hand first.

"well, john?"

"may additionally i sit down in peter's chair, as he isn't right here?"

"sit down in father's chair, john!" wendy became scandalised. "absolutely no longer."

"he isn't always clearly our father," john spoke back. "he did not even understand how a father does till i showed him."

this changed into grumbling. "we whinge of john," cried the twins. Tootles held up his hand. He was so much the humblest of them, indeed he changed into the handiest humble one, that wendy became especially gentle with him.

"i do not assume," tootles said diffidently [bashfully or timidly], "that i could be father."

"no, tootles."

as soon as tootles began, which turned into no longer very frequently, he had a stupid way of taking place.

"as i can not be father," he said closely, "i don't suppose, michael, you'll let me be infant?"

"no, i won't," michael rapped out. He was already in his basket.

"as i can't be child," tootles stated, getting heavier and heavier and heavier, "do you think i can be a twin?"

"no, indeed," responded the twins; "it's incredibly difficult to be a dual."

"as i can't be anything crucial," stated tootles, "could any of you like to look me do a trick?"

"no," all of them responded. Then at remaining he stopped. "i hadn't certainly any desire," he stated. The hateful telling broke out again.

"barely is coughing on the table."

"the twins began with cheese-cakes."

"curly is taking both butter and honey."

"nibs is talking along with his mouth complete."

"i complain of the twins."

"i complain of curly."

"i whinge of nibs."

"oh expensive, oh expensive," cried wendy, "i am certain i on occasion think that spinsters are to be envied."

she instructed them to clear away, and sat all the way down to her paintings-basket, a heavy load of stockings and every knee with a hollow in it as normal.

"wendy," remonstrated [scolded] michael, "i am too big for a cradle."

"i need to have any person in a cradle," she said almost tartly, "and you are the littlest. A cradle is such a nice homely thing to have about a house."

whilst she sewed they played around her; this type of group of satisfied faces and dancing limbs lit up by way of that romantic hearth. It had end up a very acquainted scene, this, inside the domestic underneath the ground, however we are looking on it for the closing time. There has been a step above, and wendy, you may be positive, become the first to apprehend it.

"youngsters, i hear your father's step. He likes you to fulfill him on the door."

above, the redskins crouched before peter.

"watch properly, braves. I've spoken."

after which, as so often before, the homosexual youngsters dragged him from his tree. As so often before, however never once more. He had added nuts for the men as well as the best time for wendy.

"peter, you simply smash them, you realize," wendy simpered [exaggerated a smile].

"ah, antique female," said peter, putting up his gun.

"it became me told him mothers are known as antique girl," michael whispered to curly.

"i whinge of michael," said curly immediately. The first twin got here to peter. "father, we want to bop."

"dance away, my little man," stated peter, who changed into in excessive good humour.

"however we want you to bounce."

peter become surely the great dancer among them, however he pretended to be scandalised.

"me! My old bones would rattle!"

"and mummy too."

"what," cried wendy, "the mother of such an armful, dance!"

"but on a saturday night time," barely insinuated. It changed into now not truely saturday night, as a minimum it could had been, for they'd lengthy lost remember of the days; however constantly if they wanted to do something unique they stated this become saturday night time, after which they did it.

"of path it is saturday night, peter," wendy stated, relenting.

"humans of our parent, wendy!"

"but it is handiest amongst our personal progeny [children]."

"genuine, genuine."

so they were instructed they might dance, however they must put on their nighties first.

"ah, antique lady," peter stated aside to wendy, warming himself via the fire and looking down at her as she sat turning a heel, "there is nothing extra exceptional of an nighttime for you and me when the day's toil is over than to rest by way of the hearth with the children close to by."

"it is sweet, peter, isn't it?" wendy said, frightfully gratified. "peter, i assume curly has your nose."

"michael takes after you."

she went to him and placed her hand on his shoulder.

"expensive peter," she stated, "with such a big circle of relatives, of course, i've now exceeded my first-class, however you don't want to [ex]change me, do you?"

"no, wendy."

really he did now not need a change, but he looked at her uncomfortably, blinking, you recognize, like one not certain whether he become conscious or asleep.

"peter, what is it?"

"i used to be simply wondering," he stated, a little scared. "it is only make-believe, isn't it, that i'm their father?"

"oh yes," wendy said primly [formally and properly].

"you spot," he continued apologetically, "it'd make me appear so antique to be their real father."

"but they may be ours, peter, yours and mine."

"but not really, wendy?" he asked anxiously.

"not in case you don't desire it," she replied; and she particularly heard his sigh of remedy. "peter," she asked, trying to talk firmly, "what are your precise emotions to [about] me?"

"the ones of a dedicated son, wendy."

"i notion so," she stated, and went and sat through herself at the extreme cease of the room.

"you are so queer," he said, frankly confused, "and tiger lily is just the identical. There's some thing she desires to be to me, but she says it is not my mother."

"no, indeed, it isn't always," wendy spoke back with frightful emphasis. Now we recognize why she turned into prejudiced against the redskins.

"then what is it?"

"it isn't always for a lady to tell."

"oh, thoroughly," peter said, a bit nettled. "possibly tinker bell will inform me."

"oh yes, tinker bell will let you know," wendy retorted scornfully. "she is an abandoned little creature."

right here tink, who turned into in her bedroom, eavesdropping, squeaked out some thing impudent.

"she says she glories in being deserted," peter interpreted. He had a sudden concept. "perhaps tink wants to be my mother?"

"you stupid ass!" cried tinker bell in a passion. She had said it so often that wendy wished no translation.

"i almost believe her," wendy snapped. Fancy wendy snapping! But she were lots attempted, and she little knew what become to take place earlier than the night time turned into out. If she had known she could not have snapped. None of them knew. Possibly it turned into fine not to know. Their lack of expertise gave them one more satisfied hour; and because it changed into to be their ultimate hour on the island, allow us to rejoice that there have been sixty happy minutes in it. They sang and danced of their night-robes. One of these deliciously creepy tune it turned into, wherein they pretended to be apprehensive at their personal shadows, little witting that so soon shadows would near in upon them, from whom they would decrease in actual worry. So uproariously homosexual became the dance, and how they buffeted every other at the bed and out of it! It become a pillow combat as opposed to a dance, and when it became completed, the pillows insisted on one bout extra, like companions who recognise that they will by no means meet once more. The memories they instructed, earlier than it became time for wendy's exact-night story! Even barely attempted to inform a tale that night time, but the starting was so fearfully stupid that it appalled now not best the others however himself, and he said thankfully:

"sure, it's miles a dull beginning. I say, allow us to fake that it's far the give up."

after which at closing all of them were given into bed for wendy's tale, the story they cherished quality, the story peter hated. Usually when she started to inform this tale he left the room or placed his hands over his ears; and in all likelihood if he had finished either of those things this time they might all still be on the island. However to-night he remained on his stool; and we will see what passed off.

Chapter

11

"listen, then," stated wendy, settling all the way down to her tale, with michael at her ft and seven boys within the bed. "there has been as soon as a gentleman—"

"i had alternatively he had been a lady," curly said.

"i wish he were a white rat," said nibs.

"quiet," their mother admonished [cautioned] them. "there has been a girl additionally, and—"

"oh, mummy," cried the first dual, "you suggest that there is a female also, don't you? She is not useless, is she?"

"oh, no."

"i am exceptionally happy she isn't always lifeless," said tootles. "are you satisfied, john?"

"of path i'm."

"are you satisfied, nibs?"

"alternatively."

"are you glad, twins?"

"we're happy."

"oh pricey," sighed wendy.

"little much less noise there," peter known as out, decided that she should have truthful play, however beastly a story it is probably in his opinion.

"the gentleman's call," wendy continued, "was mr. Darling, and her name was mrs. Darling."

"i knew them," john stated, to annoy the others.

"i assume i knew them," stated michael as an alternative doubtfully.

"they have been married, you understand," defined wendy, "and what do you observed that they had?"

"white rats," cried nibs, stimulated.

"no."

"it is exceedingly confusing," said tootles, who knew the story by using heart.

"quiet, tootles. That they had 3 descendants."

"what's descendants?"

"properly, you're one, dual."

"did you listen that, john? I'm a descendant."

"descendants are handiest kids," said john.

"oh expensive, oh pricey," sighed wendy. "now those three kids had a devoted nurse called nana; however mr. Darling turned into indignant with her and chained her up inside the backyard, and so all the kids flew away."

"it's an awfully accurate story," stated nibs.

"they flew away," wendy continued, "to the neverland, in which the lost kids are."

"i just idea they did," curly broke in excitedly. "i don't know how it's far, but i simply concept they did!"

"o wendy," cried tootles, "changed into one of the lost children referred to as tootles?"

"yes, he was."

"i am in a tale. Hurrah, i am in a tale, nibs."

"hush. Now i want you to recollect the feelings of the unhappy dad and mom with all their kids flown away."

"oo!" all of them moaned, although they had been now not honestly considering the emotions of the unhappy parents one jot.

"consider the empty beds!"

"oo!"

"it is exceedingly unhappy," the primary twin said cheerfully.

"i don't see how it can have a satisfied finishing," stated the second one twin. "do you, nibs?"

"i am frightfully stressful."

"in case you knew how outstanding is a mom's love," wendy instructed them triumphantly, "you'll haven't any fear." she had now come to the component that peter hated.

"i do like a mother's love," stated tootles, hitting nibs with a pillow. "do you like a mother's love, nibs?"

"i do simply," stated nibs, hitting lower back.

"you see," wendy stated complacently, "our heroine knew that the mom could constantly depart the window open for her kids to fly back by means of; so they stayed away for years and had a lovable time."

"did they ever go lower back?"

"let us now," said wendy, bracing herself up for her greatest attempt, "take a peep into the future;" and they all gave themselves the twist that makes peeps into the destiny less difficult. "years have rolled by using, and who's this fashionable female of unsure age alighting at london station?"

"o wendy, who is she?" cried nibs, every bit as excited as though he did not know.

"can or not it's—yes—no—it's miles—the fair wendy!"

"oh!"

"and who are the two noble portly figures accompanying her, now grown to guy's property? Can they be john and michael? They're!"

"oh!"

"'see, expensive brothers,' says wendy pointing upwards, 'there is the window still status open. Ah, now we are rewarded for our elegant faith in a mother's love.' so up they flew to their mummy and daddy, and pen can't describe the glad scene, over which we draw a veil."

that turned into the story, and they had been as thrilled with it because the honest narrator herself. The whole thing just as it need to be, you spot. Off we skip like the most heartless things inside the international, which is what children are, but so appealing; and we've a completely egocentric time, after which whilst we've got want of special interest we nobly go back for it, assured that we will be rewarded rather than smacked. So excellent certainly changed into their religion in a mother's love that they felt they could have enough money to be callous for a piece longer. However there was one there who knew better, and when wendy completed he uttered a hole groan.

"what's it, peter?" she cried, running to him, wondering he was unwell. She felt him solicitously, decrease down than his chest. "where is it, peter?"

"it isn't that sort of pain," peter responded darkly.

"then what type is it?"

"wendy, you are wrong about mothers."

they all accumulated spherical him in affright, so alarming was his agitation; and with a first-rate candour he instructed them what he had hitherto concealed.

"long ago," he stated, "i idea like you that my mom could always keep the window open for me, so i stayed away for moons and moons and moons, after which flew lower back; however the window became barred, for mom had forgotten all about me, and there has been some other little boy drowsing in my bed."

i'm no longer certain that this was proper, however peter thought it was authentic; and it scared them.

"are you sure moms are like that?"

"sure."

so this turned into the fact approximately moms. The toads! Nevertheless it's miles nice to be careful; and no person is aware of so quickly as a infant while he have to supply in. "wendy, allow us to [let's] move home," cried john and michael collectively.

"yes," she said, clutching them.

"no longer to-night time?" asked the lost boys bewildered. They knew in what they called their hearts that you will get on pretty properly with out a mother, and that it's far handiest the mothers who assume you can not.

"right away," wendy replied resolutely, for the horrible idea had come to her: "possibly mom is in half mourning by this time."

this dread made her forgetful of what should be peter's emotions, and she or he said to him rather sharply, "peter, will you are making the necessary preparations?"

"in case you desire it," he responded, as coolly as though she had asked him to skip the nuts. Not so much as a sorry-to-lose-you between them! If she did not thoughts the parting, he become going to reveal her, become peter, that neither did he. However of direction he cared very a whole lot; and he became so full of wrath towards grown-ups, who, as usual, had been spoiling the whole lot, that as quickly as he were given inner his tree he breathed deliberately short short breaths at the price of approximately 5 to a second. He did this because there is a saying in the neverland that, every time you breathe, a grown-up dies; and peter was killing them off vindictively as speedy as feasible. Then having given the important commands to the redskins he lower back to the home, in which an unworthy scene have been enacted in his absence. Panic-afflicted at the concept of dropping wendy the misplaced boys had advanced upon her threateningly.

"it is going to be worse than before she got here," they cried.

"we shan't permit her move."

"allow's maintain her prisoner."

"ay, chain her up."

in her extremity an instinct told her to which ones to show.

"tootles," she cried, "i attraction to you."

was it no longer extraordinary? She appealed to tootles, quite the silliest one. Grandly, however, did tootles respond. For that one second he dropped his silliness and spoke with dignity.

"i'm just tootles," he stated, "and nobody minds me. But the first who does now not behave to wendy like an english gentleman i can blood him severely."

he drew returned his hanger; and for that instantaneous his sun become at noon. The others held again uneasily. Then peter again, and they saw right now that they might get no assist from him. He could preserve no girl in the neverland towards her will.

"wendy," he said, striding up and down, "i've requested the redskins to manual you through the wood, as flying tires you so."

"thank you, peter."

"then," he continued, in the quick sharp voice of one conversant in be obeyed, "tinker bell will take you across the sea. Wake her, nibs."

nibs had to knock two times earlier than he got a solution, though tink had truely been sitting up in bed listening for some time.

"who are you? How dare you? Depart," she cried.

"you are to rise up, tink," nibs known as, "and take wendy on a adventure."

of route tink have been extremely joyful to pay attention that wendy turned into going; but she changed into jolly properly determined not to be her courier, and she stated so in nonetheless extra offensive language. Then she pretended to be asleep once more.

"she says she won't!" nibs exclaimed, aghast at such insubordination, whereupon peter went sternly towards the younger lady's chamber.

"tink," he rapped out, "if you don't rise up and dress at once i'm able to open the curtains, after which we will all see you to your negligee [nightgown]."

this made her leap to the floor. "who said i wasn't getting up?" she cried. Inside the interim the boys were observing very forlornly at wendy, now equipped with john and michael for the journey. By means of this time they had been dejected, now not simply because they were about to lose her, but additionally due to the fact they felt that she became going off to some thing fine to which they'd now not been invited. Novelty became beckoning to them as regular. Crediting them with a nobler feeling wendy melted.

"expensive ones," she stated, "if you will all come with me i feel almost certain i will get my mom and dad to undertake you."

the invitation become intended specially for peter, but every of the boys changed into questioning exclusively of himself, and straight away they jumped with pleasure.

"however may not they suppose us as a substitute a handful?" nibs requested inside the center of his jump.

"oh no," stated wendy, rapidly thinking it out, "it will most effective imply having a few beds in the drawing-room; they can be hidden in the back of the monitors on first thursdays."

"peter, can we cross?" all of them cried imploringly. They took it without any consideration that if they went he would move additionally, but without a doubt they scarcely cared. Accordingly kids are ever geared up, when novelty knocks, to wilderness their dearest ones.

"all right," peter replied with a bitter smile, and right away they rushed to get their matters.

"and now, peter," wendy said, thinking she had positioned the whole lot proper, "i'm going to present you your medication earlier than you go." she loved to present them medication, and certainly gave them an excessive amount of. Of course it became simplest water, however it become out of a bottle, and she or he always shook the bottle and counted the drops, which gave it a certain medicinal best. On this occasion, but, she did not deliver peter his draught [portion], for simply as she had prepared it, she noticed a glance on his face that made her heart sink.

"get your things, peter," she cried, shaking.

"no," he spoke back, pretending indifference, "i'm now not going with you, wendy."

"yes, peter."

"no."

to expose that her departure would go away him unmoved, he skipped up and down the room, gambling gaily on his heartless pipes. She had to run approximately after him, although it became alternatively undignified.

"to discover your mother," she coaxed. Now, if peter had ever quite had a mom, he now not overlooked her. He may want to do very well with out one. He had concept them out, and remembered only their terrible points.

"no, no," he advised wendy decisively; "perhaps she could say i was antique, and i simply need continually to be a bit boy and to have fun."

"but, peter—"

"no."

and so the others had to be instructed.

"peter isn't always coming."

peter not coming! They gazed blankly at him, their sticks over their backs, and on every stick a bundle. Their first notion become that if peter was not going he had probable modified his mind about allowing them to cross. However he became some distance too proud for that. "if you locate your mothers," he stated darkly, "i am hoping you will like them."

the awful cynicism of this made an uncomfortable impression, and most of them started to look as an alternative dubious. In the end, their faces stated, had been they not noodles to want to move?

"now then," cried peter, "no fuss, no blubbering; goodbye, wendy;" and he held out his hand cheerily, quite as if they have to truly move now, for he had some thing critical to do. She needed to take his hand, and there has been no indication that he would decide upon a thimble.

"you will recall approximately changing your flannels, peter?" she said, lingering over him. She become usually so unique about their flannels.

"sure."

"and you will take your medicinal drug?"

"yes."

that appeared to be the whole lot, and an awkward pause followed. Peter, but, became now not the kind that breaks down earlier than other humans. "are you prepared, tinker bell?" he known as out.

"ay, ay."

"then lead the manner."

tink darted up the nearest tree; but nobody followed her, for it become at this second that the pirates made their dreadful attack upon the redskins. Above, wherein all have been so nevertheless, the air changed into hire with shrieks and the clash of steel. Underneath, there has been lifeless silence. Mouths opened and remained open. Wendy fell on her knees, however her hands were extended toward peter. All arms were extended to him, as though unexpectedly blown in his direction; they have been beseeching him mutely now not to desert them. As for peter, he seized his sword, the equal he notion he had slain barbecue with, and the lust of battle became in his eye.

Chapter

12

the pirate assault had been a complete marvel: a positive evidence that the unscrupulous hook had performed it improperly, for to surprise redskins pretty is past the wit of the white man. By all of the unwritten legal guidelines of savage warfare it is usually the redskin who attacks, and with the wiliness of his race he does it simply before the sunrise, at which time he is aware of the courage of the whites to be at its lowest ebb. The white guys have inside the interim made a rude stockade on the summit of yonder undulating floor, on the foot of which a movement runs, for it is destruction to be too some distance from water. There they anticipate the onslaught, the green ones clutching their revolvers and treading on twigs, however the antique palms drowsing tranquilly until simply earlier than the dawn. Via the long black night the savage scouts wriggle, snake-like, most of the grass with out stirring a blade. The brushwood closes in the back of them, as silently as sand into which a mole has dived. Now not a sound is to be heard, save when they provide vent to a notable imitation of the lonely call of the coyote. The cry is responded by way of other braves; and a number of them do it even higher than the coyotes, who are not very good at it. So the relax hours put on on, and the lengthy suspense is horribly seeking to the paleface who has to stay thru it for the first time; however to the educated hand those ghastly calls and nevertheless ghastlier silences are however an intimation of how the night is marching. That this become the same old manner was so well known to hook that during dismissing it he can't be excused on the plea of lack of know-how. The piccaninnies, on their component, trusted implicitly to his honour, and their whole movement of the night time sticks out in marked evaluation to his. They left nothing undone that changed into regular with the popularity of their tribe. With that alertness of the senses that's immediately the surprise and depression of civilised peoples, they knew that the pirates have been at the island from the instant considered one of them trod on a dry stick; and in an exceptionally short space of time the coyote cries began. Every foot of floor among the spot wherein hook had landed his forces and the home under the trees changed into stealthily examined with the aid of braves carrying their mocassins with the heels in the front. They discovered simplest one hillock with a circulation at its base, in order that hook had no choice; here he have to set up himself and look forward to simply earlier than the sunrise. Everything being for this reason mapped out with nearly diabolical cunning, the primary body of the redskins folded their blankets around them, and inside the phlegmatic manner this is to them, the pearl of manhood squatted above the children's domestic, anticipating the cold second after they ought to deal pale death. Right here dreaming, although extensive-wakeful, of the terrific tortures to which they have been to place him at first light, those confiding savages have been determined by the treacherous hook. From the money owed afterwards supplied by way of such of the scouts as escaped the carnage, he does now not seem even to have paused on the growing floor, even though it's far positive that in that grey mild he must have seen it: no thought of ready to be attacked seems from first to remaining to have visited his subtle thoughts; he would no longer even hold off until the night was almost spent; on he pounded with no policy but to fall to [get into combat]. What ought to the bewildered scouts do, masters as they have been of each battle-like artifice save this one, however trot helplessly after him, exposing themselves fatally to view, whilst they gave pathetic utterance to the coyote cry. Around the courageous tiger lily have been a dozen of her stoutest warriors, and that they all of sudden saw the perfidious pirates bearing down upon them. Fell from their eyes then the movie via which they had checked out victory. No greater would they torture at the stake. For them the satisfied hunting-grounds become now. They knew it; but as their father's sons they acquitted themselves. Even then they'd time to accumulate in a phalanx [dense formation] that could had been difficult to break had they risen quickly, however this they were forbidden to do by using the traditions of their race. It's far written that the noble savage must by no means express surprise within the presence of the white. For that reason horrible as the unexpected look of the pirates have to were to them, they remained stationary for a second, no longer a muscle transferring; as though the foe had come with the aid of invitation. Then, certainly, the tradition gallantly upheld, they seized their weapons, and the air was torn with the war-cry; but it was now too past due. It is no a part of ours to explain what turned into a massacre rather than a combat. Consequently perished the various flower of the piccaninny tribe. Not all unavenged did they die, for with lean wolf fell alf mason, to disturb the spanish major no extra, and among others who bit the dust have been geo. Scourie, chas. Turley, and the alsatian foggerty. Turley fell to the tomahawk of the horrible panther, who in the long run cut a manner via the pirates with tiger lily and a small remnant of the tribe. To what volume hook is in charge for his techniques in this event is for the historian to determine. Had he waited on the rising floor until the proper hour he and his men would probable have been butchered; and in judging him it is only truthful to take this into account. What he need to perhaps have accomplished was to acquaint his combatants that he proposed to observe a new technique. However, this, as destroying the element of wonder, could have made his strategy of no avail, so that the complete query is beset with difficulties. One cannot at least withhold a reluctant admiration for the wit that had conceived so bold a scheme, and the fell [deadly] genius with which it became achieved. What have been his personal emotions about himself at that positive moment? Fain [gladly] would his dogs have known, as respiratory heavily and wiping their cutlasses, they accumulated at a discreet distance from his hook, and squinted via their ferret eyes at this first-rate guy. Elation should were in his heart, but his face did not replicate it: ever a darkish and solitary enigma, he stood aloof from his fans in spirit as in substance. The night time's work became now not yet over, for it was no longer the redskins he had pop out to wreck; they have been however the bees to be smoked, so that he ought to get on the honey. It become pan he desired, pan and wendy and their band, but mainly pan. Peter changed into such a small boy that one tends to surprise at the man's hatred of him. Genuine he had flung hook's arm to the crocodile, but even this and the multiplied insecurity of lifestyles to which it led, because of the crocodile's pertinacity [persistance], hardly account for a vindictiveness so relentless and malignant. The fact is that there has been a something approximately peter which goaded the pirate captain to frenzy. It changed into not his braveness, it changed into not his attractive appearance, it changed into now not—. There is no beating approximately the bush, for we realize quite well what it became, and have got to inform. It was peter's cockiness. This had got on hook's nerves; it made his iron claw twitch, and at night time it disturbed him like an insect. Even as peter lived, the tortured guy felt that he changed into a lion in a cage into which a sparrow had come. The question now was the way to get down the trees, or the way to get his dogs down? He ran his greedy eyes over them, searching for the thinnest ones. They wriggled uncomfortably, for they knew he would not scruple [hesitate] to ram them down with poles. In the interim, what of the boys? We have visible them at the primary clang of the guns, turned because it have been into stone figures, open-mouthed, all appealing with outstretched palms to peter; and we go back to them as their mouths near, and their hands fall to their aspects. The pandemonium above has ceased almost as unexpectedly as it arose, surpassed like a fierce gust of wind; but they know that in the passing it has determined their fate. Which facet had received? The pirates, listening avidly at the mouths of the bushes, heard the query positioned via every boy, and regrettably, additionally they heard peter's solution.

"if the redskins have won," he said, "they will beat the tom-tom; it's far always their signal of victory."

now smee had discovered the tom-tom, and became at that moment sitting on it. "you may in no way listen the tom-tom again," he muttered, however inaudibly of direction, for strict silence have been enjoined [urged]. To his amazement hook signed him to conquer the tom-tom, and slowly there came to smee an know-how of the dreadful wickedness of the order. By no means, possibly, had this simple man well-liked hook a lot. Twice smee beat upon the tool, after which stopped to pay attention gleefully.

"the tom-tom," the miscreants heard peter cry; "an indian victory!"

the doomed children responded with a cheer that was track to the black hearts above, and nearly at once they repeated their exact-byes to peter. This perplexed the pirates, but all their other emotions had been swallowed by means of a base pleasure that the enemy had been about to come up the timber. They smirked at every different and rubbed their fingers. Swiftly and silently hook gave his orders: one guy to each tree, and the others to arrange themselves in a line two yards aside.

Chapter

13

The more quickly this horror is disposed of the higher. The primary to emerge from his tree changed into curly. He rose out of it into the fingers of cecco, who flung him to smee, who flung him to starkey, who flung him to invoice jukes, who flung him to noodler, and so he changed into tossed from one to any other until he fell on the feet of the black pirate. All of the boys have been plucked from their timber on this ruthless way; and several of them had been within the air at a time, like bales of products flung from hand at hand. A unique treatment became accorded to wendy, who got here last. With ironical politeness hook raised his hat to her, and, supplying her his arm, escorted her to the spot wherein the others had been being gagged. He did it with such an air, he become so frightfully distingue [imposingly distinguished], that she changed into too fascinated to cry out. She was most effective a touch female. Perhaps it is tell-tale to expose that for a second hook entranced her, and we tell on her only due to the fact her slip led to bizarre effects. Had she haughtily unhanded him (and we should have cherished to put in writing it of her), she could had been hurled via the air like the others, after which hook could likely not had been present at the tying of the kids; and had he no longer been at the tying he would now not have observed barely's mystery, and with out the name of the game he couldn't currently have made his foul attempt on peter's life. They were tied to prevent their flying away, doubled up with their knees close to their ears; and for the trussing of them the black pirate had cut a rope into nine identical portions. All went well till barely's flip got here, whilst he changed into observed to be like the ones demanding parcels that use up all the string in going spherical and go away no tags [ends] with which to tie a knot. The pirates kicked him in their rage, just as you kick the parcel (though in fairness you must kick the string); and unusual to mention it turned into hook who told them to belay their violence. His lip was curled with malicious triumph. While his dogs were simply sweating due to the fact whenever they attempted to % the unhappy lad tight in one component he bulged out in every other, hook's grasp thoughts had long gone some distance below slightly's surface, probing no longer for consequences but for reasons; and his exultation confirmed that he had located them. Slightly, white to the gills, knew that hook had amazed [discovered] his mystery, which changed into this, that no boy so blown out could use a tree in which an average guy want stick. Negative slightly, most wretched of all the children now, for he was in a panic about peter, bitterly regretted what he had performed. Madly addicted to the drinking of water while he changed into warm, he had swelled in outcome to his present girth, and in preference to lowering himself to suit his tree he had, unknown to the others, whittled his tree to make it suit him. Sufficient of this hook guessed to persuade him that peter at final lay at his mercy, but no word of the dark design that now shaped in the subterranean caverns of his mind crossed his lips; he merely signed that the captives had been to be conveyed to the ship, and that he could be by myself. How to deliver them? Hunched up of their ropes they might indeed be rolled down hill like barrels, but maximum of the manner lay thru a morass. Once more hook's genius surmounted problems. He indicated that the little residence should be used as a conveyance. The children had been flung into it, four stout pirates raised it on their shoulders, the others fell in in the back of, and making a song the hateful pirate chorus the extraordinary procession set off through the timber. I don't know whether any of the children were crying; in that case, the singing drowned the sound; but because the little house disappeared inside the woodland, a brave although tiny jet of smoke issued from its chimney as if defying hook. Hook noticed it, and it did peter a bad provider. It dried up any trickle of pity for him that may have remained in the pirate's infuriated breast. The primary aspect he did on finding himself on my own inside the speedy falling night time become to tiptoe to slightly's tree, and make certain that it furnished him with a passage. Then for long he remained brooding; his hat of sick omen at the sward, so that any gentle breeze which had arisen may play refreshingly through his hair. Dark as were his thoughts his blue eyes were as tender because the periwinkle. Carefully he listened for any sound from the nether international, but all turned into as silent below as above; the house under the ground regarded to be but one more empty tenement inside the void. Changed into that boy asleep, or did he stand ready on the foot of barely's tree, together with his dagger in his hand? There has been no manner of knowing, keep by means of happening. Hook let his cloak slip softly to the floor, and then biting his lips until a lewd blood stood on them, he stepped into the tree. He become a brave guy, however for a second he had to stop there and wipe his brow, which became dripping like a candle. Then, silently, he permit himself pass into the unknown. He arrived unmolested on the foot of the shaft, and stood nonetheless again, biting at his breath, which had almost left him. As his eyes became conversant in the dim light diverse objects within the domestic below the trees took shape; however the best one on which his grasping gaze rested, long hunted for and located at ultimate, turned into the excellent mattress. At the bed lay peter speedy asleep. Unaware of the tragedy being enacted above, peter had endured, for a touch time after the kids left, to play gaily on his pipes: no doubt instead a forlorn try and prove to himself that he did no longer care. Then he decided not to take his remedy, a good way to grieve wendy. Then he lay down on the bed outside the coverlet, to vex her still extra; for she had constantly tucked them inner it, due to the fact you by no means realize that you could not grow chilly at the turn of the night time. Then he nearly cried; however it struck him how angry she would be if he laughed rather; so he laughed a haughty chortle and fell asleep within the middle of it. Now and again, although now not frequently, he had goals, and they had been more painful than the desires of different boys. For hours he couldn't be separated from those goals, though he wailed piteously in them. They needed to do, i assume, with the riddle of his lifestyles. At such instances it were wendy's custom to take him away from bed and sit down with him on her lap, soothing him in dear ways of her own invention, and whilst he grew calmer to place him again to mattress before he pretty awakened, in order that he must no longer realize of the indignity to which she had subjected him. But on this event he had fallen immediately into a dreamless sleep. One arm dropped over the edge of the bed, one leg changed into arched, and the incomplete a part of his snort turned into stranded on his mouth, which changed into open, displaying the little pearls. Hence defenceless hook discovered him. He stood silent at the foot of the tree looking across the chamber at his enemy. Did no feeling of compassion disturb his sombre breast? The person turned into not wholly evil; he loved vegetation (i've been advised) and sweet track (he changed into himself no imply performer on the harpsichord); and, permit it be frankly admitted, the idyllic nature of the scene stirred him profoundly. Mastered via his higher self he might have returned reluctantly up the tree, however for one component. What stayed him was peter's impertinent look as he slept. The open mouth, the drooping arm, the arched knee: they have been such a personification of cockiness as, taken together, will never once more, one may additionally desire, be offered to eyes so sensitive to their offensiveness. They steeled hook's heart. If his rage had broken him into a hundred pieces each one of them could have ignored the incident, and leapt at the sleeper. Though a light from the only lamp shone dimly at the bed, hook stood in darkness himself, and at the primary stealthy step forward he located an obstacle, the door of barely's tree. It did now not entirely fill the aperture, and he have been looking over it. Feeling for the catch, he discovered to his fury that it changed into low down, beyond his attain. To his disordered brain it regarded then that the worrying high-quality in peter's face and parent visibly multiplied, and he rattled the door and flung himself in opposition to it. Was his enemy to get away him after all? But what changed into that? The red in his eye had caught sight of peter's medicine standing on a ledge inside clean reach. He fathomed what it turned into straightaway, and immediately knew that the sleeper became in his power. Lest he ought to be taken alive, hook constantly carried about his person a dreadful drug, combined with the aid of himself of all the loss of life-dealing rings that had come into his possession. Those he had boiled down into a yellow liquid quite unknown to technological know-how, which turned into in all likelihood the maximum virulent poison in existence. 5 drops of this he now delivered to peter's cup. His hand shook, however it become in exultation rather than in disgrace. As he did it he prevented glancing at the sleeper, but now not lest pity ought to unnerve him; simply to keep away from spilling. Then one long gloating look he solid upon his victim, and turning, wormed his manner with issue up the tree. As he emerged at the top he appeared the very spirit of evil breaking from its hollow. Donning his hat at its maximum rakish attitude, he wound his cloak around him, protecting one lead to front as though to hide his character from the night time, of which it turned into the blackest component, and muttering surprisingly to himself, stole away through the timber. Peter slept on. The mild guttered [burned to edges] and went out, leaving the tenement in darkness; but nevertheless he slept. It need to have been no longer less than ten o'clock through the crocodile, whilst he suddenly sat up in his bed, awakened by way of he knew no longer what. It changed into a soft cautious tapping on the door of his tree. Tender and careful, but in that stillness it become sinister. Peter felt for his dagger until his hand gripped it. Then he spoke.

"who's that?"

for long there has been no answer: on the other hand the knock.

"who are you?"

no solution. He become pleased, and he loved being thrilled. In two strides he reached the door. Unlike slightly's door, it filled the aperture [opening], in order that he could not see past it, nor could the one knocking see him.

"i may not open until you speak," peter cried. Then at last the visitor spoke, in a lovely bell-like voice.

"permit me in, peter."

it become tink, and fast he unbarred to her. She flew in excitedly, her face flushed and her dress stained with dust.

"what is it?"

"oh, you may never bet!" she cried, and presented him three guesses. "out with it!" he shouted, and in one ungrammatical sentence, so long as the ribbons that conjurers [magicians] pull from their mouths, she told of the seize of wendy and the men. Peter's coronary heart bobbed up and down as he listened. Wendy certain, and at the pirate ship; she who loved the whole thing to be in order that!

"i'll rescue her!" he cried, leaping at his weapons. As he leapt he notion of some thing he could do to thrill her. He may want to take his remedy. His hand closed on the deadly draught.

"no!" shrieked tinker bell, who had heard hook mutter about his deed as he sped thru the forest.

"why not?"

"it is poisoned."

"poisoned? Who may want to have poisoned it?"

"hook."

"do not be silly. How may want to hook have were given down right here?"

regrettably, tinker bell couldn't give an explanation for this, for even she did now not realize the darkish secret of slightly's tree. Though hook's phrases had left no room for doubt. The cup became poisoned.

"besides," stated peter, pretty believing himself "i by no means fell asleep."

he raised the cup. No time for words now; time for deeds; and with certainly one of her lightning actions tink were given between his lips and the draught, and drained it to the dregs.

"why, tink, how dare you drink my medication?"

however she did not solution. Already she become reeling within the air.

"what's the matter with you?" cried peter, afraid.

"it become poisoned, peter," she informed him softly; "and now i'm going to be dead."

"o tink, did you drink it to store me?"

"sure."

"but why, tink?"

her wings would scarcely convey her now, however in respond she alighted on his shoulder and gave his nose a loving bite. She whispered in his ear "you silly ass," after which, tottering to her chamber, lay down on the mattress. His head nearly stuffed the fourth wall of her little room as he knelt close to her in distress. Every moment her mild became growing fainter; and he knew that if it went out she might be no extra. She favored his tears a lot that she placed out her lovely finger and let them run over it. Her voice become so low that in the beginning he couldn't make out what she said. Then he made it out. She became saying that she thought she could get properly once more if kids believed in fairies. Peter flung out his hands. There have been no kids there, and it changed into night time time; but he addressed all who is probably dreaming of the neverland, and who had been consequently nearer to him than you think: boys and women of their nighties, and naked papooses in their baskets hung from bushes.

"do you trust?" he cried. Tink sat up in bed nearly in a timely fashion to concentrate to her destiny. She fancied she heard solutions within the affirmative, and then again she wasn't sure.

"what do you suspect?" she requested peter.

"in case you trust," he shouted to them, "clap your palms; don't let tink die."

many clapped. A few didn't. Some beasts hissed. The clapping stopped all at once; as if countless moms had rushed to their nurseries to look what on this planet become occurring; however already tink became stored. First her voice grew strong, then she popped away from bed, then she became flashing via the room greater merry and impudent than ever. She in no way notion of thanking folks that believed, however she could have want to get at the ones who had hissed.

"and now to rescue wendy!"

the moon become riding in a cloudy heaven when peter rose from his tree, begirt [belted] with weapons and sporting little else, to set out upon his perilous quest. It turned into no longer this type of night time as he could have chosen. He had hoped to fly, retaining not far from the floor in order that not anything unwonted have to get away his eyes; but in that fitful mild to have flown low could have meant trailing his shadow thru the trees, for that reason disturbing birds and acquainting a watchful foe that he become astir. He regretted now that he had given the birds of the island such abnormal names that they may be very wild and hard of approach. There has been no different path however to press ahead in redskin fashion, at which luckily he changed into an adept [expert]. But in what course, for he could not ensure that the youngsters were taken to the ship? A mild fall of snow had obliterated all footmarks; and a deathly silence pervaded the island, as if for a area nature stood still in horror of the latest carnage. He had taught the youngsters something of the woodland lore that he had himself discovered from tiger lily and tinker bell, and knew that during their dire hour they were now not likely to forget it. Barely, if he had an possibility, might blaze [cut a mark in] the timber, as an example, curly might drop seeds, and wendy would go away her handkerchief at a few essential place. The morning changed into needed to look for such guidance, and he could not wait. The top global had known as him, however could provide no help. The crocodile surpassed him, however not any other residing aspect, not a sound, not a movement; and but he knew nicely that unexpected death might be at the following tree, or stalking him from behind. He swore this terrible oath: "hook or me this time."

> now he crawled forward like a snake, and once more erect, he darted across a space on which the moonlight played, one finger on his lip and his dagger at the ready. He turned into frightfully glad.

Chapter

14

one inexperienced light squinting over kidd's creek, that's near the mouth of the pirate river, marked where the brig, the jolly roger, lay, low in the water; a rakish-searching [speedy-looking] craft foul to the hull, each beam in her detestable, like ground strewn with mangled feathers. She changed into the cannibal of the seas, and scarce wanted that watchful eye, for she floated immune inside the horror of her call. She became wrapped within the blanket of night, through which no sound from her may want to have reached the shore. There has been little sound, and none agreeable shop the whir of the ship's stitching device at which smee sat, ever industrious and obliging, the essence of the not unusual, pathetic smee. I recognise not why he was so infinitely pathetic, until it have been because he become so pathetically ignorant of it; but even robust men had to turn rapidly from searching at him, and extra than as soon as on summer evenings he had touched the fount of hook's tears and made it waft. Of this, as of just about everything else, smee became quite unconscious. Many of the pirates leant over the bulwarks, drinking inside the miasma [putrid mist] of the night; others sprawled by way of barrels over games of dice and playing cards; and the exhausted 4 who had carried the little house lay prone at the deck, wherein even of their sleep they rolled skillfully to this side or that out of hook's reach, lest he must claw them routinely in passing. Hook trod the deck in notion. O man unfathomable. It became his hour of triumph. Peter had been removed for ever from his path, and all the different boys were in the brig, approximately to stroll the plank. It become his grimmest deed because the days whilst he had delivered barbeque to heel; and understanding as we do how vain a tabernacle is man, should we be surprised had he now paced the deck unsteadily, bellied out by means of the winds of his fulfillment? But there was no elation in his gait, which stored pace with the movement of his sombre mind. Hook became profoundly dejected. He become regularly accordingly whilst communing with himself on board deliver in the quietude of the night. It became because he became so terribly on my own. This inscrutable guy in no way felt extra by myself than whilst surrounded via his puppies. They had been socially inferior to him. Hook become no longer his authentic name. To expose who he absolutely was would even at this date set the us of a in a blaze; however as folks who examine among the traces need to already have guessed, he had been at a famous public school; and its traditions nevertheless clung to him like clothes, with which certainly they may be in large part worried. For that reason it changed into offensive to him even now to board a deliver within the identical get dressed wherein he grappled [attacked] her, and he nonetheless adhered in his walk to the college's outstanding slouch. But certainly he retained the passion for desirable shape. Properly form! However a great deal he may additionally have degenerated, he still knew that this is all that absolutely subjects. From a long way inside him he heard a creaking as of rusty portals, and thru them got here a stern faucet-faucet-tap, like hammering in the night time whilst one can't sleep. "have you ever been excellent form to-day?" became their eternal query.

"repute, fame, that glittering bauble, it is mine," he cried.

"is it quite true shape to be outstanding at something?" the tap-faucet from his college replied.

"i'm the only man whom barbeque feared," he advised, "and flint feared barbeque."

"barbecue, flint—what house?" came the slicing retort. Maximum disquieting mirrored image of all, changed into it not bad form to consider exact shape? His vitals have been tortured by way of this problem. It turned into a claw inside him sharper than the iron one; and as it tore him, the perspiration dripped down his tallow [waxy] countenance and streaked his doublet. Ofttimes he drew his sleeve throughout his face, but there has been no damming that trickle. Ah, envy now not hook. There got here to him a presentiment of his early dissolution [death]. It become as if peter's horrible oath had boarded the deliver. Hook felt a depressing choice to make his death speech, lest currently there have to be no time for it.

"higher for hook," he cried, "if he had had less ambition!" it became in his darkest hours best that he noted himself within the third character.

"no little children to love me!"

abnormal that he ought to think about this, which had never him before; perhaps the stitching system brought it to his thoughts. For long he muttered to himself, looking at smee, who turned into hemming placidly, underneath the conviction that all children feared him. Feared him! Feared smee! There has been now not a child on board the brig that night time who did now not already love him. He had stated horrid things to them and hit them with the palm of his hand, because he could not hit with his fist, but they had handiest clung to him the more. Michael had attempted on his spectacles. To inform terrible smee that they thought him cute! Hook itched to do it, however it regarded too brutal. Alternatively, he revolved this thriller in his mind: why do they locate smee lovely? He pursued the trouble like the sleuth-hound that he became. If smee turned into lovable, what become it that made him so? A terrible answer all at once offered itself—"precise form?"

had the bo'sun true shape with out understanding it, that's the nice shape of all? He remembered that you need to show you do not know you have got it earlier than you are eligible for pop [an elite social club at eton]. With a cry of rage he raised his iron quit smee's head; however he did no longer tear. What arrested him was this reflection:

"to claw a man because he is good form, what would that be?"

"awful form!"

the unhappy hook turned into as impotent [powerless] as he changed into damp, and he fell forward like a reduce flower. His puppies wondering him out of the way for a time, field immediately relaxed; and they broke into a bacchanalian [drunken] dance, which delivered him to his feet right away, all strains of human weakness gone, as though a bucket of water had surpassed over him.

"quiet, you scugs," he cried, "or i'll cast anchor in you;" and without delay the din turned into hushed. "are all the children chained, so they can not fly away?"

"ay, ay."

"then hoist them up."

the wretched prisoners have been dragged from the hold, all except wendy, and ranged in line in front of him. For a time he appeared unconscious in their presence. He lolled at his ease, buzzing, not unmelodiously, snatches of a impolite track, and fingering a percent of playing cards. Ever and anon the mild from his cigar gave a touch of colour to his face.

"now then, bullies," he stated briskly, "six of you walk the plank to-night, but i have room for 2 cabin boys. Which of you is it to be?"

"do not irritate him unnecessarily," were wendy's instructions in the keep; so tootles advanced with politeness. Tootles hated the idea of signing beneath the sort of man, but an intuition advised him that it would be prudent to lay the responsibility on an absent person; and even though a rather stupid boy, he knew that mothers on my own are always willing to be the buffer. All kids recognise this approximately mothers, and despise them for it, however make steady use of it. So tootles defined prudently, "you spot, sir, i don't assume my mom would like me to be a pirate. Would your mother like you to be a pirate, barely?"

he winked at slightly, who stated mournfully, "i don't assume so," as though he wished things have been in any other case. "could your mom like you to be a pirate, dual?"

"i do not suppose so," stated the first dual, as clever because the others. "nibs, could—"

"stow this gab," roared hook, and the spokesmen have been dragged returned. "you, boy," he said, addressing john, "you look as if you had a little pluck in you. Didst never want to be a pirate, my hearty?"

now john had now and again skilled this hankering at maths. Prep.; and he changed into struck by hook's choosing him out.

"i as soon as concept of calling myself red-passed jack," he stated diffidently.

"and a good call too. We'll call you that here, bully, in case you be part of."

"what do you watched, michael?" asked john.

"what would you name me if i join?" michael demanded.

"blackbeard joe."

michael changed into obviously impressed. "what do you watched, john?" he desired john to determine, and john wanted him to determine.

"shall we nonetheless be respectful topics of the king?" john inquired. Via hook's teeth got here the answer: "you'll must swear, 'down with the king.'"

perhaps john had not behaved very well up to now, however he shone out now.

"then i refuse," he cried, banging the barrel in the front of hook.

"and that i refuse," cried michael.

"rule britannia!" squeaked curly. The infuriated pirates buffeted them within the mouth; and hook roared out, "that seals your doom. Convey up their mother. Get the plank ready."

they have been most effective boys, and they went white as they saw jukes and cecco making ready the deadly plank. But they tried to look brave when wendy become introduced up. No words of mine can inform you how wendy despised those pirates. To the lads there was at the least a few glamour in the pirate calling; however all that she saw was that the deliver had not been tidied for years. There was now not a porthole on the dirty glass of that you might not have written together with your finger "dirty pig"; and she or he had already written it on several. But as the lads collected round her she had no thought, of direction, store for them.

"so, my beauty," stated hook, as if he spoke in syrup, "you're to peer your kids walk the plank."

pleasant gents although he turned into, the intensity of his communings had soiled his ruff, and he knew that she become staring at at it. With a hasty gesture he tried to cover it, however he turned into too late.

"are they to die?" requested wendy, with a glance of such frightful contempt that he almost fainted.

"they're," he twisted up. "silence all," he called gloatingly, "for a mother's ultimate words to her children."

at this second wendy became grand. "those are my ultimate phrases, expensive boys," she stated firmly. "i feel that i have a message to you out of your real moms, and it's far this: 'we are hoping our sons will die like english gentlemen.'"

even the pirates had been awed, and tootles cried out hysterically, "i am going to do what my mother hopes. What are you to do, nibs?"

"what my mother hopes. What are you to do, twin?"

"what my mom hopes. John, what are—"

however hook had found his voice once more.

"tie her up!" he shouted. It was smee who tied her to the mast. "see right here, honey," he whispered, "i will prevent if you promise to be my mother."

however not even for smee would she make the sort of promise. "i would nearly rather have no youngsters in any respect," she said disdainfully [scornfully]. It is sad to recognize that not a boy changed into searching at her as smee tied her to the mast; the eyes of all have been at the plank: that closing little stroll they had been approximately to take. They were not capable of hope that they could stroll it manfully, for the potential to suppose had long past from them; they may stare and shiver only. Hook smiled on them with his teeth closed, and took a step closer to wendy. His intention became to show her face so that she have to see they boys taking walks the plank one at a time. However he in no way reached her, he by no means heard the cry of suffering he was hoping to wring from her. He heard some thing else as an alternative. It turned into the horrible tick-tick of the crocodile. They all heard it—pirates, boys, wendy; and right away each head became blown in a single course; now not to the water whence the sound proceeded, however in the direction of hook. All knew that what changed into about to manifest worried him alone, and that from being actors they had been grow to be spectators. Very frightful become it to look the trade that came over him. It become as if he had been clipped at each joint. He fell in a bit heap. The sound came gradually nearer; and in advance of it came this ghastly thought, "the crocodile is set to board the ship!"

even the iron claw hung inactive; as if knowing that it changed into no intrinsic a part of what the attacking force desired. Left so fearfully alone, any other man might have lain along with his eyes close where he fell: however the massive brain of hook become nonetheless working, and below its guidance he crawled at the knees along the deck as a long way from the sound as he may want to pass. The pirates respectfully cleared a passage for him, and it become most effective when he added up towards the bulwarks that he spoke.

"conceal me!" he cried hoarsely. They gathered round him, all eyes avoided from the factor that turned into coming aboard. That they had no notion of preventing it. It changed into destiny. Only whilst hook became hidden from them did curiosity loosen the limbs of the boys so that they might rush to the ship's aspect to see the crocodile mountain climbing it. Then they got the strangest wonder of the night time of nights; for it become no crocodile that turned into coming to their resource. It become peter. He signed to them not to give vent to any cry of admiration that could rouse suspicion. Then he went on ticking.

Chapter

15

extraordinary matters happen to absolutely everyone on our way thru lifestyles without our noticing for a time that they have happened. As a consequence, to take an instance, we all at once discover that we had been deaf in one ear for we do not know how lengthy, but, say, half of an hour. Now such an revel in had come that night time to peter. While final we saw him he became stealing throughout the island with one finger to his lips and his dagger on the prepared. He had visible the crocodile skip by means of with out noticing whatever unusual approximately it, but by means of and by he remembered that it had not been ticking. At the beginning he concept this eerie, but soon concluded rightly that the clock had run down. With out giving a concept to what might be the feelings of a fellow-creature for this reason deprived of its closest associate, peter began to take into account how he may want to flip the catastrophe to his very own use; and he decided to tick, in order that wild beasts should consider he become the crocodile and let him bypass unmolested. He ticked superbly, but with one unexpected result. The crocodile turned into amongst folks who heard the sound, and it followed him, although whether with the motive of regaining what it had lost, or simply as a chum below the notion that it became again ticking itself, will by no means be surely known, for, like slaves to a fixed idea, it became a stupid beast. Peter reached the shore with out mishap, and went directly on, his legs encountering the water as though pretty unaware that they'd entered a brand new detail. As a result many animals bypass from land to water, but no different human of whom i recognise. As he swam he had however one idea: "hook or me this time." he had ticked so long that he now went on ticking without knowing that he changed into doing it. Had he known he might have stopped, for to board the brig by way of help of the tick, though an inventive idea, had not came about to him. On the contrary, he notion he had scaled her side as noiseless as a mouse; and he became amazed to peer the pirates cowering from him, with hook of their midst as abject as if he had heard the crocodile. The crocodile! No faster did peter take into account it than he heard the ticking. At the beginning he thought the sound did come from the crocodile, and he seemed in the back of him rapidly. They he realised that he was doing it himself, and in a flash he understood the scenario. "how clever of me!" he thought at once, and signed to the lads not to burst into applause. It changed into at this second that ed teynte the quartermaster emerged from the forecastle and got here alongside the deck. Now, reader, time what took place through your watch. Peter struck authentic and deep. John clapped his palms at the sick-fated pirate's mouth to stifle the dying groan. He fell ahead. Four boys caught him to prevent the thud. Peter gave the sign, and the carrion was solid overboard. There has been a splash, after which silence. How long has it taken?

"one!" (slightly had begun to be counted.)

none too soon, peter, every inch of him on tiptoe, vanished into the cabin; for multiple pirate turned into screwing up his courage to look spherical. They may pay attention each other's distressed respiratory now, which showed them that the extra terrible sound had surpassed.

"it's gone, captain," smee stated, wiping off his spectacles. "all's nevertheless once more."

slowly hook allow his head emerge from his ruff, and listened so intently that he may want to have caught the echo of the tick. There was no longer a legitimate, and he drew himself up firmly to his complete top.

"then right here's to johnny plank!" he cried openly, hating the lads extra than ever due to the fact that they had seen him unbend. He broke into the villainous ditty:

"yo ho, yo ho, the frisky plank,

you walks alongside it so,

till it goes down and also you goes down

to davy jones beneath!"

to terrorize the prisoners the extra, although with a positive loss of dignity, he danced along an imaginary plank, grimacing at them as he sang; and while he finished he cried, "do you want a hint of the cat [o' nine tails] before you walk the plank?"

at that they fell on their knees. "no, no!" they cried so piteously that each pirate smiled.

"fetch the cat, jukes," stated hook; "it is inside the cabin."

the cabin! Peter became within the cabin! The kids gazed at every different.

"ay, ay," stated jukes blithely, and he strode into the cabin. They observed him with their eyes; they scarce knew that hook had resumed his track, his dogs joining in with him:

"yo ho, yo ho, the scratching cat, its tails are 9, you realize, and while they're writ upon your back—"

what become the ultimate line will in no way be known, for of a unexpected the music was stayed by means of a dreadful screech from the cabin. It wailed via the deliver, and died away. Then was heard a crowing sound which was nicely understood by the lads, but to the pirates turned into almost greater eerie than the screech.

"what changed into that?" cried hook.

"two," said slightly solemnly. The italian cecco hesitated for a moment after which swung into the cabin. He tottered out, haggard.

"what is the problem with bill jukes, you dog?" hissed hook, towering over him.

"the matter wi' him is he's lifeless, stabbed," responded cecco in a hollow voice.

"bill jukes lifeless!" cried the startled pirates.

"the cabin's as black as a pit," cecco said, nearly gibbering, "however there is some thing terrible in there: the thing you heard crowing."

the exultation of the men, the reducing looks of the pirates, each have been seen through hook.

"cecco," he said in his maximum steely voice, "pass lower back and fetch me out that doodle-doo."

cecco, bravest of the brave, cowered before his captain, crying "no, no"; however hook changed into purring to his claw.

"did you are saying you will go, cecco?" he said musingly. Cecco went, first flinging his palms despairingly. There was no greater singing, all listened now; and once more got here a demise-screech and once more a crow. No person spoke except barely. "3," he stated. Hook rallied his dogs with a gesture. "'s'demise and odds fish," he thundered, "who is to bring me that doodle-doo?"

"wait until cecco comes out," growled starkey, and the others took up the cry.

"i suppose i heard you volunteer, starkey," stated hook, purring once more.

"no, by means of thunder!" starkey cried.

"my hook thinks you probably did," said hook, crossing to him. "i'm wondering if it'd not be recommended, starkey, to humour the hook?"

"i'll swing before i am going in there," responded starkey doggedly, and once more he had the assist of the team.

"is that this mutiny?" requested hook more pleasantly than ever. "starkey's ringleader!"

"captain, mercy!" starkey whimpered, all of a tremble now.

"shake fingers, starkey," said hook, proffering his claw. Starkey regarded round for help, however all deserted him. As he subsidized up hook superior, and now the crimson spark was in his eye. With a despairing scream the pirate leapt upon long tom and triggered himself into the ocean.

"4," said slightly.

"and now," hook stated with courtesy, "did any other gents say mutiny?" seizing a lantern and raising his claw with a menacing gesture, "i will deliver out that doodle-doo myself," he said, and sped into the cabin.

"5." how barely longed to mention it. He wetted his lips to be geared up, however hook got here awesome out, without his lantern.

"something blew out the light," he stated a bit unsteadily.

"some thing!" echoed mullins.

"what of cecco?" demanded noodler.

"he's as useless as jukes," stated hook shortly. His reluctance to go back to the cabin impressed all of them unfavourably, and the mutinous sounds once more broke forth. All pirates are superstitious, and cookson cried, "they do say the highest quality signal a deliver's accurst is while there's one on board greater than can be accounted for."

"i have heard," muttered mullins, "he continually forums the pirate craft remaining. Had he a tail, captain?"

"they say," stated another, looking viciously at hook, "that after he comes it's inside the likeness of the wickedest guy aboard."

"had he a hook, captain?" asked cookson insolently; and one after some other took up the cry, "the deliver's doomed!" at this the kids couldn't withstand elevating a cheer. Hook had properly-nigh forgotten his prisoners, however as he swung round on them now his face lit up once more.

"lads," he cried to his crew, "now here is a perception. Open the cabin door and drive them in. Let them combat the doodle-doo for their lives. In the event that they kill him, we are a lot the better; if he kills them, we are none the more severe."

for the remaining time his puppies well-known hook, and devotedly they did his bidding. The boys, pretending to struggle, were pushed into the cabin and the door changed into closed on them.

"now, listen!" cried hook, and all listened. However now not one dared to stand the door. Sure, one, wendy, who all this time were sure to the mast. It become for neither a scream nor a crow that she was watching, it turned into for the reappearance of peter. She had no longer lengthy to attend. In the cabin he had observed the component for which he had long past in search: the important thing that could unfastened the youngsters in their manacles, and now they all stole forth, armed with such guns as they might find. First signing them to hide, peter reduce wendy's bonds, and then nothing might have been simpler than for them all to fly off collectively; but one thing barred the manner, an oath, "hook or me this time." so whilst he had freed wendy, he whispered for her to hide herself with the others, and himself took her area by the mast, her cloak around him in order that he need to pass for her. Then he took a amazing breath and crowed. To the pirates it turned into a voice crying that all the men lay slain within the cabin; and that they have been panic-. Hook tried to hearten them; however like the dogs he had made them they confirmed him their fangs, and he knew that if he took his eyes off them now they might soar at him.

"lads," he said, ready to cajole or strike as want be, however never quailing for an immediately, "i've thought it out. There is a jonah aboard."

"ay," they tangled up, "a man wi' a hook."

"no, lads, no, it's the girl. Never was good fortune on a pirate deliver wi' a girl on board. We're going to right the ship whilst she's long gone."

some of them remembered that this had been a saying of flint's. "it is well worth attempting," they stated doubtfully.

"fling the lady overboard," cried hook; and they made a hurry at the determine inside the cloak.

"there may be none can save you now, missy," mullins hissed jeeringly.

"there's one," answered the figure.

"who's that?"

"peter pan the avenger!" came the terrible solution; and as he spoke peter flung off his cloak. Then all of them knew who 'twas that had been undoing them within the cabin, and twice hook essayed to talk and two times he failed. In that frightful second i suppose his fierce coronary heart broke. At closing he cried, "cleave him to the brisket!" but with out conviction.

"down, boys, and at them!" peter's voice rang out; and in every other moment the conflict of palms turned into resounding through the ship. Had the pirates saved together it is sure that they would have gained; however the onset got here after they had been nonetheless unstrung, and that they ran hither and thither, putting wildly, each wondering himself the final survivor of the team. Guy to man they had been the more potent; however they fought on the defensive simplest, which enabled the lads to seek in pairs and choose their quarry. A number of the miscreants leapt into the ocean; others hid in darkish recesses, wherein they were found via slightly, who did no longer fight, but ran about with a lantern which he flashed of their faces, so that they have been half blinded and fell as an easy prey to the reeking swords of the opposite boys. There has been little sound to be heard however the clang of guns, an occasional screech or splash, and slightly monotonously counting—5—six—seven eight—9—ten—11. I think all had been long past while a set of savage boys surrounded hook, who appeared to have a charmed lifestyles, as he saved them at bay in that circle of fireplace. They'd finished for his dogs, however this man alone appeared to be a in shape for all of them. Again and again they closed upon him, and over and over he hewed a clean space. He had lifted up one boy along with his hook, and changed into the usage of him as a buckler [shield], while some other, who had simply surpassed his sword through mullins, sprang into the fray.

"put up your swords, boys," cried the newcomer, "this man is mine."

thus hook determined himself face to face with peter. The others drew back and shaped a ring round them. For lengthy the 2 enemies looked at one another, hook shuddering slightly, and peter with the unusual smile upon his face.

"so, pan," said hook at final, "this is all your doing."

"ay, james hook," came the strict answer, "it's far all my doing."

"proud and insolent teens," said hook, "put together to fulfill thy doom."

"dark and sinister man," peter responded, "have at thee."

with out greater words they fell to, and for a space there was no advantage to both blade. Peter was a amazing swordsman, and parried with amazing rapidity; ever and anon he observed up a feint with a lunge that got beyond his foe's defence, however his shorter reach stood him in ill stead, and he could not pressure the metal domestic. Hook, scarcely his inferior in brilliancy, but now not quite so nimble in wrist play, compelled him back by way of the burden of his onset, hoping unexpectedly to stop all with a fave thrust, taught him lengthy ago with the aid of barbeque at rio; however to his astonishment he discovered this thrust grew to become aside again and again. Then he sought to close and deliver the quietus together with his iron hook, which all this time were pawing the air; however peter doubled beneath it and, lunging fiercely, pierced him inside the ribs. On the sight of his own blood, whose ordinary colour, you don't forget, became offensive to him, the sword fell from hook's hand, and he changed into at peter's mercy.

"now!" cried all the boys, however with a superb gesture peter invited his opponent to pick up his sword. Hook did so instantly, but with a tragic feeling that peter changed into showing excellent form. Hitherto he had thought it became a few fiend fighting him, however darker suspicions assailed him now.

"pan, who and what artwork thou?" he cried huskily.

"i am adolescents, i am pleasure," peter responded at a challenge, "i am a bit chook that has broken out of the egg."

this, of route, become nonsense; but it became proof to the unhappy hook that peter did no longer recognize in the least who or what he was, that's the very top of excellent shape.

"to't again," he cried despairingly. He fought now like a human flail, and each sweep of that horrible sword might have severed in twain any man or boy who obstructed it; but peter fluttered round him as if the very wind it made blew him out of the chance sector. And time and again he darted in and pricked. Hook changed into fighting now without hope. That passionate breast not asked for lifestyles; but for one boon it craved: to peer peter show awful form before it changed into bloodless all the time. Abandoning the fight he rushed into the powder magazine and fired it.

"in mins," he cried, "the ship will be blown to portions."

now, now, he notion, real form will show. But peter issued from the powder magazine with the shell in his fingers, and frivolously flung it overboard. What kind of form changed into hook himself displaying? Inaccurate man though he become, we can be satisfied, without sympathising with him, that in the end he became proper to the traditions of his race. The opposite boys were flying around him now, flouting, scornful; and he staggered about the deck putting up at them impotently, his mind turned into now not with them; it become slouching in the playing fields of long in the past, or being despatched up [to the headmaster] for properly, or looking the wall-sport from a well-known wall. And his footwear have been proper, and his waistcoat become right, and his tie was proper, and his socks have been proper. James hook, thou no longer wholly unheroic discern, farewell. For we've come to his last second. Seeing peter slowly advancing upon him thru the air with dagger poised, he sprang upon the bulwarks to cast himself into the ocean. He did not understand that the crocodile turned into expecting him; for we purposely stopped the clock that this knowledge is probably spared him: a touch mark of admire from us at the give up. He had one ultimate triumph, which i suppose we want now not grudge him. As he stood at the bulwark looking over his shoulder at peter gliding through the air, he invited him with a gesture to apply his foot. It made peter kick in place of stab. At closing hook had were given the boon for which he craved.

"horrific shape," he cried jeeringly, and went content material to the crocodile. As a consequence perished james hook.

"seventeen," barely sang out; however he turned into now not quite correct in his figures. Fifteen paid the penalty for his or her crimes that night; but two reached the shore: starkey to be captured via the redskins, who made him nurse for all their papooses, a despair come-down for a pirate; and smee, who henceforth wandered approximately the world in his spectacles, creating a precarious dwelling via pronouncing he turned into the most effective guy that jas. Hook had feared. Wendy, of direction, had stood with the aid of taking no part within the combat, though watching peter with glistening eyes; however now that every one changed into over she became prominent once more. She praised them similarly, and shuddered delightfully when michael confirmed her the area wherein he had killed one; and then she took them into hook's cabin and pointed to his watch which changed into placing on a nail. It stated "1/2-beyond one!"

the lateness of the hour changed into almost the biggest aspect of all. She were given them to bed inside the pirates' bunks pretty quick, you will be sure; all but peter, who strutted up and down on the deck, till at closing he fell asleep through the aspect of lengthy tom. He had considered one of his goals that night time, and cried in his sleep for a long term, and wendy held him tightly.

Chapter

16

via three bells that morning they were all stirring their stumps [legs]; for there was a big sea jogging; and tootles, the bo'sun, changed into among them, with a rope's result in his hand and chewing tobacco. All of them donned pirate garments cut off at the knee, shaved neatly, and tumbled up, with the authentic nautical roll and hitching their trousers. It want not be said who became the captain. Nibs and john have been first and second mate. There has been a girl aboard. The rest have been tars [sailors] earlier than the mast, and lived within the fo'c'sle. Peter had already lashed himself to the wheel; however he piped all arms and added a brief cope with to them; said he was hoping they might do their obligation like gallant hearties, but that he knew they had been the scum of rio and the gold coast, and if they snapped at him he would tear them. The bluff strident phrases struck the be aware sailors understood, and they cheered him lustily. Then some sharp orders had been given, and they turned the ship round, and nosed her for the mainland. Captain pan calculated, after consulting the deliver's chart, that if this weather lasted they should strike the azores approximately the twenty first of june, and then it would shop time to fly. Some of them desired it to be an honest deliver and others were in favour of retaining it a pirate; but the captain dealt with them as puppies, and they dared now not explicit their desires to him even in a spherical robin [one person after another, as they had to cpt. Hook]. Instant obedience turned into the simplest secure aspect. Slightly got a dozen for searching confused while instructed to take soundings. The overall feeling changed into that peter turned into sincere simply now to lull wendy's suspicions, but that there is probably a change whilst the new match became geared up, which, against her will, she was making for him out of some of hook's wickedest clothes. It became afterwards whispered amongst them that on the first night he wore this in shape he sat long inside the cabin with hook's cigar-holder in his mouth and one hand clenched, all but for the forefinger, which he bent and held threateningly aloft like a hook. In place of looking the ship, but, we need to now return to that desolate home from which 3 of our characters had taken heartless flight so long ago. It appears a shame to have overlooked no. 14 all this time; and but we may be certain that mrs. Darling does not blame us. If we had lower back quicker to appearance with sorrowful sympathy at her, she would in all likelihood have cried, "don't be silly; what do i rely? Do go back and maintain an eye fixed at the kids." so long as moms are like this their children will take gain of them; and they will lay to [bet on] that. Even now we mission into that familiar nursery best because its lawful occupants are on their way home; we're simply hurrying on earlier of them to look that their beds are nicely aired and that mr. And mrs. Darling do not exit for the night. We aren't any more than servants. Why on the planet have to their beds be well aired, since they left them in this type of thankless hurry? Would it not not serve them jolly well right in the event that they got here returned and discovered that their parents were spending the week-give up within the u . S .? It'd be the moral lesson they have been in need of ever seeing that we met them; but if we contrived things in this manner mrs. Darling might in no way forgive us. One aspect i ought to love to do immensely, and that is to tell her, inside the way authors have, that the children are coming lower back, that indeed they may be here on thursday week. This will wreck so absolutely the surprise to which wendy and john and michael are searching ahead. They had been planning it out on the deliver: mother's rapture, father's shout of joy, nana's jump through the air to include them first, when what they ought to be prepared for is a good hiding. How scrumptious to break all of it by breaking the news earlier; so that when they input grandly mrs. Darling might not even provide wendy her mouth, and mr. Darling can also exclaim pettishly, "sprint all of it, right here are those boys once more." but, we must get no thank you even for this. We're beginning to recognise mrs. Darling through this time, and may be certain that she could upbraid us for depriving the kids in their little satisfaction.

"but, my expensive madam, it is ten days till thursday week; in order that through telling you what's what, we will prevent ten days of disappointment."

"sure, however at what a price! By depriving the youngsters of ten mins of pride."

"oh, if you examine it in that way!"

"what other manner is there in which to have a look at it?"

you spot, the female had no right spirit. I had meant to say pretty best matters about her; however i despise her, and not one in all them will i say now. She does no longer really want to be told to have matters ready, for they're geared up. All of the beds are aired, and she or he never leaves the residence, and have a look at, the window is open. For all of the use we are to her, we'd nicely move back to the deliver. However, as we are right here we may also as properly live and appearance on. That is all we are, lookers-on. No one sincerely wants us. So allow us to watch and say jaggy matters, within the desire that a number of them will harm. The only change to be visible in the night time-nursery is that between nine and 6 the kennel is no longer there. While the kids flew away, mr. Darling felt in his bones that every one the blame turned into his for having chained nana up, and that from first to closing she have been wiser than he. Of path, as we've visible, he turned into pretty a easy guy; indeed he would possibly have handed for a boy again if he were able to take his baldness off; but he had additionally a noble experience of justice and a lion's braveness to do what regarded right to him; and having notion the matter out with aggravating care after the flight of the children, he went down on all fours and crawled into the kennel. To all mrs. Darling's pricey invitations to him to pop out he spoke back alas but firmly:

"no, my own one, this is the location for me."

inside the bitterness of his regret he swore that he would in no way depart the kennel till his youngsters came back. Of path this became a pity; however anything mr. Darling did he needed to do in excess, in any other case he quickly gave up doing it. And there in no way turned into a extra humble man than the once proud george darling, as he sat inside the kennel of an night speakme together with his spouse of their kids and all their quite ways. Very touching became his deference to nana. He would no longer permit her come into the kennel, but on all other topics he observed her desires implicitly. Each morning the kennel was carried with mr. Darling in it to a cab, which conveyed him to his workplace, and he again domestic within the same manner at six. Some thing of the strength of character of the person might be visible if we consider how touchy he was to the opinion of neighbours: this guy whose each movement now attracted surprised interest. Inwardly he need to have suffered torture; however he preserved a calm outside even when the young criticised his little domestic, and he usually lifted his hat politely to any female who looked inner. It can were quixotic, but it was impressive. Soon the inward which means of it leaked out, and the brilliant heart of the public became touched. Crowds observed the cab, cheering it lustily; captivating ladies scaled it to get his autograph; interviews appeared inside the higher class of papers, and society invited him to dinner and added, "do come in the kennel."

on that eventful thursday week, mrs. Darling changed into in the night-nursery watching for george's go back domestic; a completely unhappy-eyed female. Now that we examine her closely and do not forget the gaiety of her within the antique days, all long past now simply because she has misplaced her babes, i discover i won't have the ability to mention nasty things approximately her in spite of everything. If she changed into too keen on her rubbishy kids, she could not help it. Take a look at her in her chair, in which she has fallen asleep. The nook of her mouth, in which one seems first, is sort of withered up. Her hand moves restlessly on her breast as though she had a pain there. A few like peter nice, and some like wendy great, but i love her first-class. Assume, to make her satisfied, we whisper to her in her sleep that the brats are coming again. They are clearly inside two miles of the window now, and flying sturdy, but all we want whisper is that they may be on the manner. Permit's. It is a pity we did it, for she has started up, calling their names; and there may be nobody within the room but nana.

"o nana, i dreamt my dear ones had come lower back."

nana had filmy eyes, but all she ought to do changed into placed her paw gently on her mistress's lap; and they had been sitting collectively accordingly whilst the kennel become introduced returned. As mr. Darling places his head out to kiss his spouse, we see that his face is extra worn than of yore, however has a softer expression. He gave his hat to liza, who took it scornfully; for she had no creativeness, and turned into quite incapable of expertise the reasons of one of these man. Out of doors, the group who had accompanied the cab home had been nevertheless cheering, and he was clearly not unmoved.

"concentrate to them," he said; "it's far very fulfilling."

"masses of little boys," sneered liza.

"there had been several adults to-day," he confident her with a faint flush; however when she tossed her head he had no longer a word of reproof for her. Social success had now not spoilt him; it had made him sweeter. For some time he sat along with his head out of the kennel, speakme with mrs. Darling of this fulfillment, and pressing her hand reassuringly whilst she stated she hoped his head could now not be turned through it.

"however if i were a susceptible guy," he said. "desirable heavens, if i had been a weak guy!"

"and, george," she said timidly, "you are as complete of remorse as ever, are not you?"

"full of remorse as ever, dearest! See my punishment: living in a kennel."

"however it's far punishment, isn't always it, george? You are sure you aren't taking part in it?"

"my love!"

you may be sure she begged his pardon; after which, feeling drowsy, he curled round within the kennel.

"won't you play me to sleep," he asked, "on the nursery piano?" and as she became crossing to the day-nursery he delivered thoughtlessly, "and close that window. I experience a draught."

"o george, in no way question me to do that. The window ought to always be left open for them, always, continually."

now it changed into his turn to beg her pardon; and he or she went into the day-nursery and played, and soon he was asleep; and whilst he slept, wendy and john and michael flew into the room. Oh no. We've written it so, because that was the charming association planned through them earlier than we left the deliver; however something have to have passed off when you consider that then, for it is not they who have flown in, it is peter and tinker bell. Peter's first phrases tell all.

"quick tink," he whispered, "near the window; bar it! It's right. Now you and that i must get away by the door; and when wendy comes she can assume her mom has barred her out; and she will should cross again with me."

now i apprehend what had hitherto confused me, why whilst peter had exterminated the pirates he did not go back to the island and leave tink to escort the kids to the mainland. This trick were in his head all of the time. As opposed to feeling that he became behaving badly he danced with glee; then he peeped into the day-nursery to see who was playing. He whispered to tink, "it is wendy's mother! She is a pretty girl, but now not so quite as my mom. Her mouth is complete of thimbles, but not so complete as my mom's become."

of direction he knew nothing anything approximately his mother; but he every now and then bragged about her. He did now not realize the song, which was "domestic, sweet home," but he knew it was announcing, "come lower back, wendy, wendy, wendy"; and he cried exultantly, "you may by no means see wendy once more, girl, for the window is barred!"

he peeped in once more to see why the music had stopped, and now he saw that mrs. Darling had laid her head at the container, and that two tears were sitting on her eyes.

"she desires me to unbar the window," notion peter, "but i might not, no longer i!"

he peeped once more, and the tears had been nonetheless there, or any other had taken their location.

"she's awfully fond of wendy," he stated to himself. He turned into irritated together with her now for not seeing why she could not have wendy. The cause became so simple: "i am fond of her too. We cannot both have her, female."

however the girl might not make the nice of it, and he was sad. He ceased to examine her, but even then she would no longer allow cross of him. He skipped about and made funny faces, but whilst he stopped it turned into just as if she had been inside him, knocking.

"oh, all right," he stated at closing, and gulped. Then he unbarred the window. "come on, tink," he cried, with a frightful sneer on the laws of nature; "we do not need any stupid mothers;" and he flew away. For this reason wendy and john and michael located the window open for them in the end, which of route was more than they deserved. They alighted on the ground, pretty unashamed of themselves, and the youngest one had already forgotten his domestic.

"john," he stated, looking around him doubtfully, "i assume i've been right here before."

"of course you've got, you stupid. There is your antique mattress."

"so it's far," michael stated, but no longer with plenty conviction.

"i say," cried john, "the kennel!" and he dashed throughout to look at it.

"possibly nana is inside it," wendy stated. However john whistled. "hullo," he said, "there's a person internal it."

"it's father!" exclaimed wendy.

"let me see father," michael begged eagerly, and he took a good appearance. "he is not so massive because the pirate i killed," he stated with such frank disappointment that i am satisfied mr. Darling became asleep; it would were sad if the ones have been the primary phrases he heard his little michael say. Wendy and john had been stunned particularly at locating their father within the kennel.

"in reality," said john, like person who had lost religion in his reminiscence, "he used no longer to sleep inside the kennel?"

"john," wendy stated falteringly, "possibly we don't bear in mind the vintage life in addition to we concept we did."

a kick back fell upon them; and serve them right.

"it's far very careless of mom," said that young scoundrel john, "no longer to be here whilst we come lower back."

it become then that mrs. Darling began playing once more.

"it's mom!" cried wendy, peeping.

"so it is!" said john.

"then are you no longer in reality our mother, wendy?" asked michael, who became simply sleepy.

"oh dear!" exclaimed wendy, with her first real twinge of regret [for having gone], "it was quite time we got here lower back."

"allow us to creep in," john suggested, "and placed our fingers over her eyes."

but wendy, who saw that they ought to smash the joyous information extra lightly, had a better plan.

"allow us to all slip into our beds, and be there whilst she comes in, just as if we had in no way been away."

and so while mrs. Darling went lower back to the night-nursery to look if her husband become asleep, all the beds were occupied. The children waited for her cry of pleasure, but it did not come. She noticed them, but she did now not accept as true with they were there. You spot, she saw them of their beds so frequently in her dreams that she notion this become simply the dream putting round her still. She sat down in the chair by the fire, in which in the antique days she had nursed them. They couldn't apprehend this, and a chilly worry fell upon all the 3 of them.

"mother!" wendy cried.

"it is wendy," she stated, however nevertheless she turned into positive it was the dream.

"mother!"

"that is john," she stated.

"mother!" cried michael. He knew her now.

"it really is michael," she said, and he or she stretched out her palms for the three little selfish kids they would by no means envelop once more. Yes, they did, they went spherical wendy and john and michael, who had slipped out of bed and run to her.

"george, george!" she cried whilst she should talk; and mr. Darling woke to proportion her bliss, and nana got here dashing in. There couldn't were a lovelier sight; but there was none to look it besides a bit boy who become staring in at the window. He had had ecstasies innumerable that different children can by no means realize; but he turned into looking through the window at the one joy from which he should be for ever barred.

Chapter

17

I am hoping you need to recognize what have become of the opposite boys. They have been waiting under to provide Wendy time to explain about them; and when they had counted five hundred they went up. They went up by using the stair, because they thought this would make a better impression. They stood in a row in front of Mrs. Darling, with their hats off, and wishing they had been no longer wearing their pirate clothes. They said nothing; however their eyes requested her to have them. They have to have looked at Mr. Darling also, however they forgot about him. Of route Mrs. Darling said at once that she could have them; but Mr. Darling became curiously depressed, and that they saw that he considered six an alternatively large number.

"I should say," he said to Wendy, "which you do not do things by using halves," a grudging commentary which the twins idea changed into pointed at them. The first dual changed into the proud one, and he asked, flushing, "do you believe you studied we need to be too much of a handful, sir? Due to the fact, if so, we can go away."

"Father!" Wendy cried, bowled over; however nonetheless the cloud was on him. He knew he was behaving unworthily, but he could not assist it.

"We could lie doubled up," stated nibs.

"I always cut their hair myself," said Wendy.

"George!" mrs. Darling exclaimed, pained to see her pricey one displaying himself in such an negative light. Then he burst into tears, and the fact got here out. He changed into as happy to have them as she become, he stated, but he notion they need to have asked his consent in addition to hers, instead of treating him as a cypher [zero] in his own house.

"i do not think he's a cypher," tootles cried instantly. "do you think he is a cypher, curly?"

"no, i do not. Do you believe you studied he is a cypher, slightly?"

"rather not. Dual, what do you think?"

it grew to become out that no longer one among them notion him a cypher; and he became absurdly gratified, and stated he could discover area for all of them inside the drawing-room if they geared up in.

"we're going to match in, sir," they assured him.

"then follow the leader," he cried gaily. "thoughts you, i am no longer certain that we've a drawing-room, but we fake we've, and it's all of the same. Hoop los angeles!"

he went off dancing via the residence, and they all cried "hoop la!" and danced after him, searching for the drawing-room; and that i forget about whether or not they discovered it, but at any rate they observed corners, and all of them equipped in. As for peter, he saw wendy once again before he flew away. He did no longer exactly come to the window, but he brushed against it in passing so that she may want to open it if she appreciated and get in touch with to him. That's what she did.

"hullo, wendy, good-bye," he said.

"oh pricey, are you going away?"

"yes."

"you do not feel, peter," she said falteringly, "which you would really like to say whatever to my parents approximately a very sweet issue?"

"no."

"approximately me, peter?"

"no."

mrs. Darling got here to the window, for at present she was preserving a sharp eye on wendy. She told peter that she had followed all of the different boys, and would like to undertake him also.

"could you send me to highschool?" he inquired craftily.

"sure."

"and then to an office?"

"i assume so."

"quickly i'd be a person?"

"very quickly."

"i do not want to go to high school and learn solemn things," he instructed her passionately. "i do not need to be a man. O wendy's mom, if i used to be to awaken and feel there was a beard!"

"peter," said wendy the comforter, "i ought to love you in a beard;" and mrs. Darling stretched out her palms to him, however he repulsed her.

"keep again, lady, nobody is going to catch me and make me a man."

"however where are you going to stay?"

"with tink in the house we constructed for wendy. The fairies are to put it excessive up many of the tree tops wherein they sleep at nights."

"how lovely," cried wendy so longingly that mrs. Darling tightened her grip.

"i thought all the fairies had been useless," mrs. Darling stated.

"there are always loads of young ones," explained wendy, who turned into now quite an authority, "due to the fact you see while a brand new child laughs for the first time a brand new fairy is born, and as there are always new infants there are constantly new fairies. They live in nests on the tops of timber; and the mauve ones are boys and the white ones are women, and the blue ones are simply little sillies who aren't sure what they're."

"i shall have such amusing," stated peter, with eye on wendy.

"it'll be as an alternative lonely within the evening," she said, "sitting via the hearth."

"i shall have tink."

"tink cannot pass a 20th part of the way spherical," she reminded him a bit tartly.

"sneaky inform-story!" tink called out from somewhere round the corner.

"it would not depend," peter said.

"o peter, you are aware of it matters."

"properly, then, include me to the little residence."

"may also i, mummy?"

"truely no longer. I've got you home again, and that i suggest to maintain you."

"however he does so want a mom."

"so do you, my love."

"oh, all right," peter stated, as though he had requested her from politeness merely; but mrs. Darling saw his mouth twitch, and he or she made this handsome provide: to allow wendy go to him for every week each 12 months to do his spring cleansing. Wendy could have favored a more permanent association; and it seemed to her that spring could be long in coming; but this promise despatched peter away pretty gay again. He had no sense of time, and changed into so full of adventures that every one i've advised you about him is simplest a halfpenny-worth of them. I suppose it became because wendy knew this that her remaining words to him have been those instead plaintive ones:

"you won't forget about me, peter, will you, before spring cleaning time comes?"

of route peter promised; after which he flew away. He took mrs. Darling's kiss with him. The kiss that were for no person else, peter took pretty without difficulty. Funny. But she regarded satisfied. Of path all of the boys went to highschool; and most of them got into class iii, however slightly turned into placed first into magnificence iv and then into elegance v. Class i is the pinnacle class. Earlier than they'd attended college a week they saw what goats they had been no longer to remain at the island; however it turned into too overdue now, and soon they settled all the way down to being as regular as you or me or jenkins minor [the younger jenkins]. It's far sad to have to say that the strength to fly gradually left them. At the beginning nana tied their feet to the bed-posts so they must now not fly away in the night; and one among their diversions by way of day was to faux to fall off buses [the english double-deckers]; however by using and with the aid of they ceased to drag at their bonds in bed, and determined that they harm themselves once they let pass of the bus. In time they could not even fly after their hats. Need of exercise, they called it; however what it certainly supposed become that they not believed. Michael believed longer than the other boys, although they jeered at him; so he become with wendy whilst peter came for her on the cease of the first yr. She flew away with peter inside the frock she had woven from leaves and berries in the neverland, and her one worry was that he would possibly word how brief it had come to be; however he by no means observed, he had a lot to mention about himself. She had seemed ahead to thrilling talks with him approximately antique times, but new adventures had crowded the vintage ones from his thoughts.

"who is captain hook?" he asked with interest whilst she stated the arch enemy.

"don't you take into account," she requested, amazed, "the way you killed him and saved all our lives?"

"i forget about them once i kill them," he responded carelessly. When she expressed a doubtful wish that tinker bell would be glad to peer her he said, "who's tinker bell?"

"o peter," she said, stunned; but even if she explained he couldn't remember.

"there are such plenty of them," he stated. "i expect she is no greater."

i count on he was proper, for fairies don't live lengthy, however they're so little that a brief time appears a very good even as to them. Wendy become pained too to find that the past year turned into but as the day before today to peter; it had seemed the sort of lengthy yr of waiting to her. However he become exactly as captivating as ever, and that they had a lovely spring cleansing inside the little house at the tree tops. Next yr he did no longer come for her. She waited in a brand new frock because the antique one truly could no longer meet; but he in no way got here.

"perhaps he's ill," michael said.

"you understand he's in no way sick."

michael came near her and whispered, with a shiver, "perhaps there may be no such individual, wendy!" after which wendy could have cried if michael had now not been crying. Peter got here next spring cleansing; and the odd issue turned into that he by no means knew he had ignored a yr. That become the final time the girl wendy ever saw him. For a little longer she tried for his sake now not to have developing pains; and she felt she was unfaithful to him while she got a prize for widespread information. But the years got here and went without bringing the careless boy; and once they met again wendy become a married girl, and peter changed into no more to her than a touch dust within the container in which she had saved her toys. Wendy changed into grown up. You want now not be sorry for her. She become one among the type that likes to grow up. Ultimately she grew up of her very own unfastened will a day faster than different women. All of the boys had been grown up and carried out for with the aid of this time; so it's miles scarcely really worth even as announcing whatever extra approximately them. You can see the twins and nibs and curly any day going to an office, each carrying a bit bag and an umbrella. Michael is an engine-motive force [train engineer]. Barely married a female of identify, and so he have become a lord. You see that judge in a wig coming out on the iron door? That was once tootles. The bearded man who does not recognize any tale to tell his kids changed into as soon as john. Wendy became married in white with a red sash. It is abnormal to assume that peter did no longer alight in the church and forbid the banns [formal announcement of a marriage]. Years rolled on again, and wendy had a daughter. This ought no longer to be written in ink but in a golden splash. She turned into referred to as jane, and continually had an unusual inquiring look, as if from the instant she arrived at the mainland she desired to invite questions. When she turned into old sufficient to invite them they have been ordinarily about peter pan. She cherished to pay attention of peter, and wendy advised her all she ought to bear in mind in the very nursery from which the famous flight had taken place. It changed into jane's nursery now, for her father had bought it at the 3 consistent with cents [mortgage rate] from wendy's father, who changed into not keen on stairs. Mrs. Darling turned into now lifeless and forgotten. There have been most effective beds in the nursery now, jane's and her nurse's; and there has been no kennel, for nana additionally had handed away. She died of antique age, and on the give up she had been alternatively difficult to get on with; being very firmly satisfied that no one knew how to look after youngsters except herself. Once per week jane's nurse had her nighttime off; after which it changed into wendy's part to put jane to mattress. That changed into the time for memories. It became jane's invention to raise the sheet over her mother's head and her personal, this making a tent, and inside the lousy darkness to whisper:

"what will we see now?"

"i don't assume i see something to-night time," says wendy, with a sense that if nana have been right here she would item to similarly communication.

"yes, you do," says jane, "you notice while you were a little lady."

"that is a long time in the past, sweetheart," says wendy. "ah me, how time flies!"

"does it fly," asks the artful toddler, "the manner you flew whilst you had been a touch woman?"

"the manner i flew? Do you understand, jane, i every now and then wonder whether or not i ever did genuinely fly."

"sure, you did."

"the pricey vintage days once i could fly!"

"why cannot you fly now, mother?"

"due to the fact i'm grown up, dearest. Whilst humans develop up they forget the manner."

"why do they forget about the manner?"

"due to the fact they are now not gay and harmless and heartless. It's far handiest the gay and innocent and heartless who can fly."

"what's homosexual and harmless and heartless? I do desire i have been gay and harmless and heartless."

or possibly wendy admits she does see something.

"i do believe," she says, "that it is this nursery."

"i do agree with it's miles," says jane. "go on."

they're now launched into the extremely good journey of the night time when peter flew in seeking out his shadow.

"the foolish fellow," says wendy, "attempted to stick it on with cleaning soap, and when he couldn't he cried, and that woke me, and i sewed it on for him."

"you have overlooked a piece," interrupts jane, who now knows the story better than her mother. "when you noticed him sitting on the ground crying, what did you assert?"

"i sat up in bed and i stated, 'boy, why are you crying?'"

"yes, that turned into it," says jane, with a large breath.

"after which he flew us all away to the neverland and the fairies and the pirates and the redskins and the mermaid's lagoon, and the home under the ground, and the little residence."

"sure! Which did you like nice of all?"

"i think i preferred the home beneath the ground great of all."

"yes, so do i. What become the ultimate thing peter ever said to you?"

"the remaining aspect he ever stated to me became, 'just continually be expecting me, after which a few night time you will pay attention me crowing.'"

"yes."

"however, alas, he forgot all about me," wendy stated it with a grin. She was as grown up as that.

"what did his crow sound like?" jane requested one night.

"it became like this," wendy said, seeking to imitate peter's crow.

"no, it wasn't," jane stated gravely, "it turned into like this;" and she or he did it ever a lot higher than her mom. Wendy changed into a little startled. "my darling, how can ?"

"i regularly hear it when i'm snoozing," jane said.

"ah yes, many girls listen it when they're sleeping, however i was the best one that heard it wakeful."

"fortunate you," said jane. And then one night time came the tragedy. It was the spring of the year, and the tale have been advised for the night time, and jane became now asleep in her bed. Wendy became sitting on the ground, very close to the hearth, as a way to see to darn, for there has been no different light within the nursery; and whilst she sat darning she heard a crow. Then the window blew open as of antique, and peter dropped in on the floor. He changed into precisely the same as ever, and wendy noticed at once that he nevertheless had all his first tooth. He became a touch boy, and she become grown up. She huddled by means of the hearth not bold to move, helpless and responsible, a massive girl.

"hullo, wendy," he stated, not noticing any distinction, for he became questioning mainly of himself; and in the dim light her white get dressed might have been the nightgown wherein he had seen her first.

"hullo, peter," she answered faintly, squeezing herself as small as feasible. Some thing inside her turned into crying "female, girl, let move of me."

"hullo, wherein is john?" he asked, unexpectedly missing the 1/3 bed.

"john isn't here now," she gasped.

"is michael asleep?" he asked, with a careless look at jane.

"yes," she spoke back; and now she felt that she was unfaithful to jane as well as to peter.

"that is not michael," she said quick, lest a judgment ought to fall on her. Peter appeared. "hullo, is it a brand new one?"

"sure."

"boy or girl?"

"girl."

now definitely he could understand; however no longer a piece of it.

"peter," she stated, faltering, "are you awaiting me to fly away with you?"

"of direction; that is why i've come." he introduced a touch sternly, "have you ever forgotten that this is spring cleansing time?"

she knew it became vain to mention that he had allow many spring cleaning times skip.

"i can not come," she said apologetically, "i have forgotten the way to fly."

"i will quickly educate you once more."

"o peter, do not waste the fairy dust on me."

she had risen; and now at final a fear assailed him. "what is it?" he cried, shrinking.

"i will flip up the light," she stated, "and then you could see for yourself."

for nearly the most effective time in his existence that i realize of, peter was afraid. "do not turn up the light," he cried. She let her palms play in the hair of the tragic boy. She became not a bit lady coronary heart-damaged approximately him; she become a grown woman smiling at it all, but they were moist eyed smiles. Then she became up the light, and peter saw. He gave a cry of pain; and while the tall lovely creature stooped to lift him in her fingers he drew returned sharply.

"what is it?" he cried once more. She had to tell him.

"i'm vintage, peter. I am ever so much more than twenty. I grew up lengthy in the past."

"you promised no longer to!"

"i couldn't help it. I'm a married girl, peter."

"no, you're now not."

"sure, and the little lady inside the mattress is my child."

"no, she's no longer."

however he intended she changed into; and he took a step toward the sound asleep toddler along with his dagger upraised. Of route he did not strike. He sat down on the ground as an alternative and sobbed; and wendy did no longer recognise the way to comfort him, even though she should have executed it so effortlessly as soon as. She became best a female now, and he or she ran out of the room to try to think. Peter endured to cry, and soon his sobs woke jane. She sat up in bed, and changed into interested straight away.

"boy," she stated, "why are you crying?"

peter rose and bowed to her, and he or she bowed to him from the bed.

"hullo," he stated.

"hullo," stated jane.

"my name is peter pan," he told her.

"yes, i realize."

"i came back for my mom," he defined, "to take her to the neverland."

"sure, i understand," jane stated, "i've been looking forward to you."

when wendy returned diffidently she determined peter sitting on the mattress-submit crowing gloriously, even as jane in her nighty turned into flying spherical the room in solemn ecstasy.

"she is my mom," peter defined; and jane descended and stood by way of his facet, with the look in her face that he favored to see on girls when they gazed at him.

"he does so need a mother," jane stated.

"sure, i recognize." wendy admitted instead forlornly; "no one is aware of it so nicely as i."

"goodbye," said peter to wendy; and he rose in the air, and the shameless jane rose with him; it became already her simplest way of transferring approximately. Wendy rushed to the window.

"no, no," she cried.

"it's far just for spring cleaning time," jane said, "he desires me continually to do his spring cleansing."

"if most effective i may want to go together with you," wendy sighed.

"you notice you can't fly," stated jane. Of direction ultimately wendy let them fly away together. Our closing glimpse of her suggests her at the window, looking them receding into the sky until they have been as small as stars. As you observe wendy, you may see her hair turning into white, and her discern little again, for all this occurred long in the past. Jane is now a common grown-up, with a daughter known as margaret; and every spring cleansing time, except whilst he forgets, peter comes for margaret and takes her to the neverland, wherein she tells him memories approximately himself, to which he listens eagerly. Whilst margaret grows up she will have a daughter, who's to be peter's mom in flip; and thus it will cross on, as long as youngsters are homosexual and innocent and heartless.

Printed in Great Britain
by Amazon